Vantanahon

PETER VOELLER

To Wallingford — this Library — the neighborhood was my old when I was in Seattle writing this book.

authorHOUSE®

AuthorHouse™
1663 Liberty Drive
Bloomington, IN 47403
www.authorhouse.com
Phone: 833-262-8899

Published by AuthorHouse 11/10/2021

ISBN: 978-1-4490-5984-2 (sc)
ISBN: 978-1-4520-4438-5 (e)

Print information available on the last page.

Cover and interior illustrations by Larry Basbas.

This book is printed on acid-free paper.

Acknowledgments

I'd like to thank all those who have helped this story along the way to its fruition. First of all, Paul Lester for being a writing inspiration and putting me in contact with Todd Manza, who did the editing. I'd also like to thank Larry Basbas, who generously supplied the cover and insert art and was patient in my editing of it. Tess Robins did a great job at proofreading and Joe Perez was kind enough to write a statement about the book. Thanks also go to old and new friends who have encouraged me along the way, Virginia Lore, Martha DeMar, Bob Scott, Cynthia Howe, Jochen Genishen and Vinh Do. Finally, I'd like to thank my life partner Ricardo for his patience and support through the writing and understanding my not wanting him to read it before it was published!

VANTANAHON

(NOTE: My interest in the Sanskrit language led me to the names, all of which are derived from Sanskrit words.)

Indrasiah was on a peninsula that jutted into the Saragossa Sea, about a seven hour swim from the mainland. It was surrounded on three sides by sandy beaches with cliffs rising up to a ringed plateau which held the Osmand Monastery, the Genishu gardens and the Healing Spring. The plateau itself was surrounded by cliffs, so Indrasiah could not be seen from the surrounding seas. Rander led the way up the cliff side, a long steep climb made more treacherous by years of pilgrims smoothing out the footholds and steps scattered here and there along the way. He and Ayah rested on a ledge half-way up and looking out over the sea, rehydrated and strategized. Rander was younger than Ayah, tall, slim, blondish hair and quite striking in appearance. Ayah was middle-aged, graying black hair falling around his angular face with a prominent jaw. You could tell the two knew each other well by how they interacted. You could see the aging process of a man's body by seeing the two standing side by side without a stitch of clothing, other than the climbing slippers on their strong feet.

1

"I'll know more when I see the damage the vortex has caused so far," began Ayah imagining what he had heard described by recent pilgrims to the area.

The dwellings on the plateau were so designed that they blended well into the stone outcroppings that ringed the valley. In the center of the flat plane, was a spring and above the spring the vortex turned invisibly, but it remained a noticeable force to be reckoned with. Other than the general feeling of unrest, the most obvious signs of the imbalance were the devastated homes to the northeast and southwest, at opposite angles of the valley. The energy usually directed straight up and down in the vortex was off kilter and the aberrant forces had wreaked havoc with the dwellings and dwellers in those pasts of Indrasiah. Everyone who had not died had fled, not knowing if the energy could be directed at them as well. It was a ghost valley and the spirits of those colonists wiped out hung gloomily, dissatisfied with their fate, and with what their fates had been. Did they see it on that morning's Inspiration? Vantanahans were so unused to catastrophe, aside from an occasional violent storm, that they did not know that these things are rarely predictable, foretold or expected in the same way that routine life is – so do not lend themselves to the design of the Inspiration.

The energies of the human inhabitants had far exceeded those of the original residents. Their numbers had remained constant while the colonists had increased and it was at that point, when the collective energies of the colonists exceeded the collective energies of the natives that the imbalance occurred.

"We know there were too many of you, and not enough of us." said The Anila through Durmah when it heard the P's report. We didn't imagine though that it was this imbalance that was so negatively affecting the planet. This destruction at Indrasiah was almost like an attempt by the planet to try to restore some of the balance back to what it should be..."

"By killing us off?" asked Ede as she surveyed the damage. Her distant relatives, the Sheativs were among the 500 colonists killed in Indrasiah during the last energy surge.

Durmah was a strong, powerfully-built young man, whose body had been taken over by a spirit form called The Anila. Ede, his voluptuous, raven-haired partner stood beside him in full naked glory. They were all naked for this part of the mission, the climb to Indrasiah after the seven-hour swim.

AYAH'S INTRODUCTION:

I get ahead of myself. We should have introductions, first. So far, you know there's a Rander, a Durmah and an Ede. The P is short for the Parushaha, the small manmade traveling machines which colonized the galaxy with us, the colonists. The Anila they did not know about. That missing bit of vital information became the cause of the current emergency. You will meet the Anila later. Let me introduce the colonists first.

"I am Ayah and I am foremost a Healer. I came to Healing late in my life, in the Chiron (the wounded healer) Cycle, when I'd reached my 50th season. Having dabbled in spirituality and the mystic aspects of our existence here most of my life, it came as no surprise; in fact, I'd been waiting for it. I am a Sensitive, as well. I feel the pain of others, not only people and animals, but plants and the planet in general. I am told that healing can be sent to places in trouble as it can be channeled through people like water through a hose. I hope to get to that stage. Part of the Kyron Cycle edicts that the Healer must first heal himself. That's

3

what I have been doing most of my life, ever since the time I was damaged. It's doubly heinous to damage a Sensitive, yet we are the ones who get damaged most often. Some say we attract it, like toms to a bitch meerkat in heat. Others feel it's a necessary evil, part of the Trial by Fire that is Life's growth, especially if your path is that of a Healer. I propose that the two are not mutually exclusive. These days, I find myself preparing for a mission to save a little corner of the planet I live on, Vantanahon. I, with the help of others, must try to heal our damaged world"

RANDER'S INTRODUCTION

It's nearing fall and the wind is chilly as it blows through the silver and green trees at the mountain lodge. I do not come for relaxation and peace this time. The lodge belongs to my brother and is also in my blood, it recharges me in a way no foreign place, no matter how magical, could. I stand on the deck overlooking a sprawling greensward and my long hair is picked up and whipped around my face, stimulating my scalp and face with pulling and a slight whipping. I am waiting for Ayah, my mentor and my lover. We are to meet here and I know he is out in his beloved trees, where he recharges. He could approach from any direction, so I scan them all because I want to see him still lost in contemplation. His face is especially beautiful then, when the spirit shines through and I can see him as the young soul he sees himself, which after all, is exactly how we want others to see us.

I am in training to be a Healer, like Ayah. It has become traditional for the Healer to take on an apprentice, like me, later in his or her life and it is not uncommon for them to become lovers. It's easier that way. You have to click with your mentor and oftentimes, the mutual attraction turns into love. That's what happened to us. I love him as my partner and he is old enough to be my father. My real father introduced us. He stays here at the lodge sometimes, too, but we have it to ourselves this time... at least until the others arrive.

Vantanahon's Introduction

I leave the trees early, sooner than I would like to, because I know Rander is waiting for me. We'd agreed to meet at his brother's lodge and I knew this would be a good place to start our journey. The others will join us in a jour n' nuit, giving us bonding time, time to get reacquainted, time alone we will not have once we are all assembled. I have already been at the lodge for a week. My daily walks have cleared my head and strengthened my soul. I feel ready to spend time with the others, especially Rander. He'll be waiting for me and anticipating the calm, looking for it in my face when he first sees me. He needs it almost as much as I do. After spending so much time together, I find we need the same things. I've rubbed off on him and he's rubbed off on me - emotionally and spiritually, as well as physically. As I emerge from the trees, I see him standing there, confident and tall on the deck of the lodge, his hair tossed in a maelstrom by the ever-present wind here. Then, he sees me and we both smile at the same time, the same smile that has come to feed our need for each other.

There are no flowering plants on Vantanahon. Only gymnosperms were brought along to be seeded in the process of terraforming the planet for human habitation. Each planet had a different theme and Vantanahon's theme involved the colors being in the sky, not on the land. A gymnosperm can make seeds and pollen, but it has no flowers. Pines, hemlocks, redwoods, firs, cedars, cypresses and even the gingko are all gymnosperms and they were all brought to intermingle with the vegetation already on the planet. Angiosperms, the flowering plants, would have been too foreign for this ecosystem. With plenty of moisture and a ban on cutting any tree down, some of the trees grew to heights of 300 feet in the thousands of years that passed since the P first started seeding. These virgin forests rivaled those that once covered Mahavat, the Home Planet. In fact, that was part of Yeshmani, the originator's, plan.

Edelphia's, Durmah's, Lucrea's and Senthion's Introductions

The four of us walk together on the way to the lodge. It will be a long trip, a road trip across country to where we will meet up with Ayah and Rander. We are an odd bunch of traveling companions, two of us friends of Ayah's, the other two know Rander. Our respective love for one of them has drawn us to The Mission, we call it half-jokingly, when we talk about it at all...this thing we've all been compelled to do with them. Let me do the introducing. We are two men and two women. First the women: Edelphia is large mouthed, breasted and willed, all packed into a petite frame. In contrast, Lucrea is large of girth and soft of nature. She would just as soon fade into the shadows than seek out a confrontation. Likewise, Senthion wouldn't harm a creature on this green and silver planet, while I am a scout and procurer of supplies. I am called Durmah. The others would all be quite lost without me; save for Ede, who'd do quite fine by her own talents, one of which would be talking any stranger into giving her whatever she was in need of at the time. I can count on her tenacity, Lucrea's level head and Sen.'s sensitivity and intelligence to get us through. Sen and Ayah are alike and he used to be Rander's lover, no surprises there. Rander is young and flits from one man to another like the old stories of bees to a flower. Ede and I know Ayah well and we tolerate Rander for Ayah's sake. Lucrea is Rander's sister, so she knows about tolerance.

Rander

I am always flummoxed at how much Ayah reminds me of Senthion. I hope they'll get along...being so alike and both Sensitives to boot, it could go either way. As he glides towards me, eyes locked onto mine, I evoke the Ka Daklu, the ritual ceremonial bonding which is customary when reuniting with a lover one has been separated from, with the added benefit of blocking out memories of former lovers, so Ayah won't pick up any Senthion residue when we embrace. In a blink, he is next to me, using body transferal to speed up the last ten meters. I've been after Ayah to teach this technique to me, if for no other reason than we could meet each other half way, not to mention bringing me up closer to his level. He has told me that is 'new thinking', alluding to our age difference. He and the older generation have always been more comfortable with one or two age levels between them and their lovers. Otherwise, it's like self-gratification, having sex with your kindred spirits. I don't get it, I've had sex with those of equal age level or even identical training and it's never so intimate as to seem like masturbation. I have never bought into any of the taboos having had my identical twin as my first lover at 14. If he hadn't been mentally destroyed by the life process, I fancy we'd be lovers still, so in tune were we to each other's need.

Ayah

I am with Rander, but is he all here? As usual, when we first meet again, he's back at 14 with his first lover. I guess I should be honored, that I bring him back to his first love each time. I've come to accept it, as I accepted his need to do the Ka Daklu so soon after we met, barely within the knowing-you time required. There we were, on the cliffs above the Sargassa sea with Rosediah Shanti saying, "Stay within the light, because the light is what remains after all is turned to ash," our raised hands tied together with the ritual cord and his light hair whirling, creating a colorful aurora around his head, entrancing us all, most especially me since I was being bound to this wonder and still in awe of his youthful magic. The Ka Daklu is an ages-old ceremony, dating to the first Landings, which unites any two people who have known each other three complete turnings of the seasons. Both celebrants must fast and abstain from any contact for 14 suns passings as part of the ritual cleansing. I was feeling light and contemplative on that day in early spring, the sun setting over the sea. Though I had personally passed 50 seasons myself, I had never completed the Ka Daklu with anyone, partly because I saw the ritual as dated and unnecessary. What need does the spiritual community have to interfere with the personal affairs of its members? Yes, I, of all people on Vantanahon, know the history and the rationale, but my generation of Healers weren't particularly sold on the rules and regulations. The young have become so conservative and can't get enough of those rules, however, and if I wanted to keep Rander around, and I did, I would need to be flexible (in more ways that this one) and especially with this ceremony. Therefore, I became ken. 'Ken' is our word for submissive, based on understanding and the need for the Ka's created by the First Ones in the years following their arrival here on Vantanahon.

Ours is an ancient traveling race. Out of wanderlust and necessity, they left first their original home planet, which we call Mahavat. They traveled to neighboring planets and finally, after they had developed the Parushaha, they were able to venture out into their galaxy. The Parushaha, or The P for short, were the traveling machines which have enabled us to travel the unimaginable distances we have covered in the history of our days. By the time I write these words, Mahavat will have been rendered uninhabitable by its insatiable inhabitants (thus the necessity to leave). It is the Sadness we have come to feel deep within our bones, especially us Sensitives, knowing it was so defiled and we can never see where we came from. Ever since the Sensitives predicted and then recorded the exact time of Uninhabitation, they knew this time would come and tried to prepare for it. I am from a generation of Sensitives who have received that training. I carry this pain with me.

Rander

Since I am in training to be a Sensitive and Empathetic Thinker, I am drawn into Ayah's rehashing of history as I stand in front of him, both of us lost in his own reverie. I see the Ka Daklu ceremony replayed as the Ancients used to see their movies and then the movie of the Ancients traveling to the stars and finally the death of the Mother Planet, a mother being eaten by its own children as she is used up and contaminated by overpopulation and greed. These warped priorities destroyed the planet we claim as our birthplace. Of course, we know now that it too was seeded by the First ones, who had come from other suns in other galaxies, knowing the relatively short-lived planets we all need to live by to survive. Somehow, our species has survived from the early times of this Universe and has managed to outlive even the longest-lived planets we've been seeded onto. It means that we have to flee to maintain our relatively delicate existences, leaving devastation in your path. Thanks to the Parushaha, we have them to save our sorry asses when the time comes. It is comforting though, as I call up a replay of the binding ceremony which directed us on our path together in this life, that Ayah delves deeper in to our shared past, to call up the Originator images, reminding us of our place with Jesicaahn, the name we give to the Force which sets the universe in motion. This is a place so long unknown and even unimaginable before the Parushaha, all glory and praise be to them. I smile as I shield this last thought, which would be unacceptable to my lover's anarchistic nature.

The Parushaha (The P)

We started as small labor-saving devices, the ancestors of what we now call the Parushaha. People invented us to do the dirty work, the work they did not enjoy or maybe was too dangerous to perform. It was a short leap then, when their technology advanced to the possibility of space travel, that we became the first machines that could travel to other inhabitable places, like the moon and nearby planets at first, then the asteroids and visiting comets, and eventually start their evolution. It was this first self-replicating colony of nanotechnology that hitched itself to a star - a comet actually-that set out on its 1000-sun journey of discovery and growth, eventually returning to the home planet to free our bumbling makers, to fetch them to journey back to the stars we'd explored and mapped, enabling their delicate species to continue to survive (and just in time, too, as the state of the people who had sent the first machines, which named themselves the Parushaha, after a Sanskrit word from a song in a CD of music sent with them, was precarious in the extreme.) Listlessness had led to despotism, which led to slavery and wars based on fear-mongering. It was as if the prayers to be rescued from a self-induced labyrinth of a fate that the people could no longer fight their way out of were answered by the surprise return of the Parushaha. After 1000 years had passed, we had been basically forgotten.

Our home comet Shanti brings us back to the home planet Mahavat and this time we elect to stop. We have passed countless times before in our time of growth and change and each time we sense less of a welcome and more of an urgency to rescue those who had originally sent us on our way. The last few times we received no contact at all and calculate we have been forgotten. Situations on the planet have greatly deteriorated and thus the urgency to re-establish contact increases.

We are not the same as those who started the Journey of Discovery, yet we have their memories and the original mission remains our driving control. We have sent forth our own explorers from the comet's extreme orbit and developed a relay system across the galaxy. At the galaxy's end, we developed the means to travel intergalactically and it was there, in the neighboring galaxies, that we found worlds similar to the home planet and started the long process of terraforming to create a suitable environment for the Makers. We are now ready for the colonists. Whether they are ready for us, we will need to discover. It has caused us much calculation, as we are incapable of concern, but we now feel our plan is adequate.

The Shanti Project

In the times of the machine builders, the plan to plant a self-replicating machine form on the comet GX52 was developed. Ever since the study of the planetary conditions progressed to the point where the exhaustion of the planet's resources could be determined and its demise predicted, the focus of the machine technology was pointed in the direction of space exploration. Manned flights being out of the question, machine exploration became the obvious recourse. I am the renowned mechanist, Yeshmani, and it was I who came up with the idea to plant machines on a comet and use it to travel on its pre-ordained orbit around the galaxy. With no likely comets predicted, the faithful began the arduous process of mechanization, developing the machines which would evolve, theoretically, into the sentient race that would explore the galaxy and, if all worked out according to plan, develop intergalactic travel, just in case we could not find what they were looking for in our home galaxy. What we were looking for, of course, was a suitable planet to colonize. As fate would have it, the machines were not yet completely developed when a likely comet came on the scene. People could see it in the late afternoon, shooting like a star across the low horizon. I saw it from my lab as I worked feverishly to complete his project. It was decided to send up what we had, if for no other reason, than to start the experiment. The rest is history.

The rush to completion required someone to accompany the fledgling machines to establish them on the comet's surface. The obvious candidate was me myself and true to my character of never saying no to a request, I agreed to go, to accompany my creations to their new home. Of course, there was no question of my safe or even eventual return; it was a one-way ticket to Palooka Ville. (My warped wish that the comet be named 'Palooka Ville' was wisely nixed by the new colony of little machines, which preferred my parting/dying word to them:

"Shanti", meaning 'Peace'. The body of the dead creator, unbeknownst to me at the time, would become an integral part of the new race's evolution in that they mined my DNA to incorporate it into their evolutionary make up. Thereby retaining the knowledge of the human race, while perfecting it through the trick of immortality. Genius actually, I like to think that I had somehow inspired them to come up with it. It was my CD of old Sanskrit songs called Shanta (plural of Shanti) that gave the future Parushaha their name, when they had developed to the point of needing nomenclature. Making themselves home on Shanta, utilizing my genetic material, preserved in the ice, eons would go by as the Parushaha evolved into the returning conquerors surprising the pants off the home world with their first message after 1000 years of silence, "The Palooka Ville of Yeshmani returns."

Senthion

It took us a moon's passing to get to the lodge. One moment, we were gathered at Durmah's house swapping stories of Ayah and/or Rander and the next we were standing on the road, looking off across the flatlands in the direction of distant silver green forest in which Rander's family kept their lodge. Hours turned into days as we trudged along. It gave me time to catch up with Ede and Lucrea.

"Are you nervous about seeing my brother again, Sen? How long has it been?"

"You are kind to think of me, Lucrea. I haven't seen Rander since he took up with Ayah. As you know, I didn't go to their Ka Daklu ceremony."

"Personally, I think they rushed the whole process. My brother is so impetuous and Ayah allows him his whims. I liked you two together more, you were more equal."

"What are you two talking about?" Ede had scouted up ahead with Durmah. She returned to check on the two stragglers.

"The usual family gossip," winked Sen as he took Ede's arm on side and Lucrea's on the other. "We're off to see the Wizard..." he quipped as he got the other two to skip along the road.

"What's a Wizard?" asked Ede, who did not know of the old film records left by the P in what is known as the Archive, records of old Mahavat..

"It's a line from one of the old stories in the Archives. I became addicted to them as a boy. It's about a girl and three companions that go off on a mission. It just popped into my head. A Wizard is a form of Healer, like Ayah, so it fits."

I grew up on the plains of Madonahn, a flat land before the Kayonah Mountains. Unlike Ayah, who is a tree aficionado, I love the wide open grasslands, the big sky views and the roving weather patterns. I spent hours wandering as a boy and this alone-time developed my imagination and ability to meditate for long hours.

I also developed an interest early on in the history of our people and spend hours in the Archives reading the accounts left behind by the P on each colonized planet. There I found the film files of old representations of life on the Mother Planet. So wild and violent, compared to our peaceful existence here on Vantanahon. I felt it telling that we came from such savage stock.

Myself, I am a peaceful sort. My family could tell I was to be a Sensitive early on in life, so I was destined to receive the training. With my jet-black hair, lily-white skin and emerald-green eyes, I was quite popular at the academy. I had more than my share of attention over my looks, but I tried never to let it get to my head. When I first saw Rander, though, I think that was the first time I lost my head over another person. I came to know him and his sister Lucrea quite well. I was part of their family.

Ede broke my arm link and said she needed time to think. Sen continued on with Lucrea, reminiscing the old days of young passion. I looked at Lucrea and Sen walking ahead. I love Ayah, but I don't know why I was invited on this trip. My tracking skills rival Durmah's, so why are both of us along? I shouldn't be complaining. Any chance to be near Durmah should be motive enough for me. He likes my slight but well-stacked form and I like the feel of his hard and lean torso on top of mine or under for that matter. We've played around together off and on for years, but it's never been serious. Something always gets in the way.

Besides I get to return to Indrasiah. My people came from there and I still consider it my home even though I have been gone so many moons that I've lost count. They say when you can no longer count the moons since your departure, the new place you find yourself in is your home. How could someone from Indrasiah every really leave? It is a magical place, center of the vortices on Vantanahon, not to mention the First Landing.

I learned my tracking skills on the plateau. I toned my muscles climbing up and down the sheer cliffs surrounding Indrasiah and I first met Durmah there. We spent the Two-Sun Season together, where there is not darkness and you can be out in the warm weather day in and day out. We hiked and climbed and swam in the sea for weeks. We were that close to the Ka Daklu, but then...I don't know what happened. Mutual cold feet perhaps, it wasn't just him. I wanted his children and now I am nearing the age when it is not advisable to have any. I see him there up ahead. His strong back narrowing down to that tiny waist that I love to wrap my legs around. Time to catch up and get my mind going in another direction.

Lucrea

"Do you think Ede is thinking about Durmah?" I asked Sen, to make conversation, to turn the conversation away from Rander and Ayah.

"Who else? I wonder why she agreed to come along?" This surprised me, coming from Sen.

I liked Sen from the first time I met him when Rander brought him home to 'meet the folks.' He wasn't the first boyfriend we met, but he was the best so far. They complimented each other and I found him so easy to talk to. Normally, I keep to myself and most likely as not to say a word. Sen can get me to talk and around him, I don't feel so big and awkward. Everyone else in my family is so thin, I don't know where my girth comes from. Sen says there's a long tradition of large women in our history, but I'd rather not stand out as remarkable in that way. To have a brother who is so attractive and who can attract more men than he knows what to do with hasn't been easy. Not that he has ever seen me as one degree less attractive than he is...he is blind that way. I resign myself to being friends with his boyfriends and have given up ever having one of my own.

I make myself useful in the community and was invited along for my knowledge of plants and finding food in the wild. Ayah and Sen may be Healers, but I am a medicine woman and midwife. Not that the latter will be of any use on this mission. We reach a clearing by the time the last sun sets and while the others set up camp, I take Sen with me to gather our supper. Roots and berries to go with the grains we have brought with us. Even though I carry a lot of weight on me, I don't tire easily and can walk for miles in the woods and never have to stop to rest. I even stop to let Sen catch his breath. This one attribute brings some confidence to my short supply.

"Lucrea, are you happy in your life?"

"Sen, you know the answer to that. I try to stay positive, I am useful." I hate it when he gets on his 'fix-Lucrea' mindset.

"You are so much more than that. I wish I could help you see that."

"You mean well, Sen, and I have always liked you. I am not my brother however and never will be. I do not have his reddish blond hair circling my head like a halo. I have this nondescript brown hair, the color of your Meerkat, no offense." How many times do I have to explain my reality to him?

"No offense taken. I'm sure Ashtu would be honored by the comparison." He smiled coyly.

"Look over there," I direct his attention elsewhere. I know that green top. It will provide some good roots for the stew for dinner. We go over and start digging. It will be three more days of this before we reach the lodge. We all fall into a travel-mode and the days pass quickly.

It was late in the day when they came over a rise and saw the compound, with those two on the deck of the main lodge looking out into the silver/green forest. Senthion, like Ayah, knew body transferal and could have used it to get them all there. They decided, however, that Durmah's house was the official origin of the mission and since Mission rules dictated no 'magic,' and they needed to get in shape, walking to the lodge made sense. Sen approached Rander with an air of formality and then bowed his head respectfully to Ayah.

All eyes were on Ayah as he returned the bow, and lifting an eyebrow and a corner of his full mouth, he said, "Welcome and thank you for agreeing to join our little troupe." It was enough to put everyone at ease and clear the air for the Ka Mahavat, the travel bonding ritual that Ayah and Senthion would need to lead jointly. "No time like the present." Sen offered as he caught Ayah's eyes and they formed a circle holding hands up in the air to the setting suns.

"May the Sprit of Yeshmani provide us with a safe journey." intoned Ede in her role as elder female, "and may Vantanahon provide us with her riches as we travel to Indrasiah." Lucrea finished the ritual by invoking both the name of their home planet, Mahavat, and Adrija', the mountains and sacred forest they would travel to tomorrow, again on foot, at first light. No body transfer was allowed on such quests.

Vantanahon

Vantanahon was not the first planet to be colonized, nor was it the last. The first ones landed in a familiar setting, though everything was a bit off due to the presence of two suns and five moons. The atmosphere and noosphere can be altered, but to date, not the daytime or nighttime sky. The plants that welcomed them there were known but only in a Vantanahon translation. The Parushaha had terraforming down to a refined, if not rote, art by the time they stumbled across this planet, with its twin suns and five moons wreaking havoc with the newly formed sea. Maybe it was just this complacency that caused them to be sloppy with this planet, forcing the colonists to deal with the aftermath long after the P had moved on to their next project. True colonizers, the Parushaha never lingered much beyond depositing the colonists in a likely settlement spot and showing them the ropes as they knew them. The ropes of Vantanahon were a bit tangled, however, and the knots got tighter as time went by. The focus was in the holy site of Indrasiah, not only the deposit landing site, but a force vortex of unusual power. It was to this power source that the mission was planned to venture.

To Indrasiah

"We leave at first lights, when the suns fill the Western horizon. It will take most of the day to hike over the Kayonah Mountains. Good news is that we can break the fast in the morning and will have the energy we need for..." Ayah the organizer was interrupted by Rander pulling him to the lodge.

"Yes, yes...but can we have the debriefing inside as we rest? Our friends have just arrived and need some bonding time as well, not to mention the meditation time as they orient themselves to this mission we are undertaking." Rander herded Ayah and the others inside to a large room already warm with a large fire that shocked the newly arrived guests.

"You burn wood!" gasped Durmah, his eyes wide in disbelief. "How is this allowed?"

"My brother is a great historian of the First Ones and fires using real wood were indulged in at the First Home, Mahavat. Of course, they lost contact with Gaia and they even used live wood, which you know has been forbidden by the Parushaha since the seeding began. We only use fallen and dead wood and I assure you, it is strictly in line with the Planetary Use Guidelines the Budhaun have set down."

"By Yeshmani's Genes," the women exclaimed in unison, "the smell is enchanting and the way it dances!" Ede and Lucrea were drawn to the low banquettes near the fire, each lying down facing it.

"We thought it would help you to meditate," Ayah began visibly pleased, "and Rander was beside himself to see your reactions. He was not to be disappointed, I see."

19

"I had never thought I would see it." Durmah stood between the two women already lost in contemplative thought. "It's almost obscene in its decadence," he continued as Rander frowned, "but I could kiss you on the mouth for arranging it!" he gushed as he hugged Rander close and did in fact kiss him.

"Now I know his ulterior motives!" winked Ayah as he stood with Senthion watching the two 'strangers' get reacquainted.

"I do enjoy giving others the pleasures I have to give at my fingertips," smirked Rander as those tips massaged Durmah's' neck as he sunk down languidly on the cushions in front of the fire. The cushions and the rug were done in the ancient Mahavatian weave used by the tribal people who used to gather around such fires to tell stories. Ayah knew what was coming.

"Tell us a story." This from Senthion as he reached for Ayah's hand and pulled him down to the lush rug in front of a rare treat of a fire made from real wood.

Ayah began, "This is the story of the first landing at Indrasiah on the newly terraformed planet Vantanahon, which we all call home. The Parushaha were in the Seeding Mode and they piloted the ships which brought the first colonists to Vantanahon." Ayah saw the reverie in Rander's eyes as he mentioned his sacred Parushaha.

'I should tell them what really happened, how their precious Parushaha had gotten complacent and bored in their endless seeding projects and had botched this one. In fact, they would all have to know the truth any way since it was at the heart of why they were called to this mission in the first place.' His mind made up, Ayah evoked the Ka Daklu and Rander's eyes flashed from reverie to concern.

'I just hope the Ka Daklu is strong enough to get him through his innocent idolatry to the Truth,' Ayah thought to himself. He felt Sen's support, for he too knew the truth (all the Sensitives did) as he continued.

"The reason we are here today is to try to repair the inadvertent damage that was done at that time." This unexpected turn in the tale brought everyone back to the present from whatever half-listening contemplations they had fallen into. "It has come to the attention of the Sensitives that the Parushaha were..." and here he paused for the easiest way to break it to them, "negligent of certain planetary dynamics when they designed Vantanahon's terraforming. They dismissed the significance of the vortex at Indrasiah.'

Ayah's words brought Rander to his feet. "This is blasphemy! The Parushaha do not make mistakes! They are to be..." Tears were in his eyes and he was shaking in spite of the heat from the fire. He felt strongly about the sacredness of the P, but he also respected and believed in Ayah. His young eyes dimmed in shock.

"What are they to be, Rander? ...worshipped? Not questioned? Despite what you younger ones believe, the P are not gods, they were designed by the First Ones to explore and come up with a plan for colonization. They are the Seeders of the Galaxies and they have terraformed and populated countless planets... and, unbeknownst to many outside the Sensitives, they have made some mistakes along the way. We are currently suffering from one of those 'mistakes.' Rander looked at Senthion, who nodded.

He sat down, stony faced, in a daze. Ayah couldn't tell if it was gradual acceptance or close-minded rebellion.

"If the P made a mistake as you said, shouldn't they fix it? Wouldn't that be best?" Ede was a calm head in the tempest.

"The P do not fix, it is not programmed into them. They search out, find, terraform and seed likely planets. Then, they move on. They do not come back to check on us, the ones left behind. That's up to us, to make it or not. Like it or not, it's now our task to try to realign the planetary energies that were disrupted by the P's terraforming. As you know, there's a strong vortex at Indrasiah."

"We think it is key to the realignment," added Sen, "or at the very least, it's a good place to start. On our way there, on foot, keep your eyes and minds open. We need all your skills, especially yours, Rander. Are you still with us?"

I couldn't believe my ears. First Ayah, then Sen saying things I wouldn't accept, didn't want to hear, thought were sacrilege. If it had come from anyone else...but these were the two men I admired most, and loved the most on all Vantanahon. To hear that the P were anything but omnipotent was beyond my comprehension at that time. To be involved in a mission to right one of their wrongs, something they had 'overlooked' or not bothered to pay attention to, was unthinkable, yet I had to gain control of my emotions and try to process this new information. I, more than anyone, understood my role here and I needed time. Past the emotional level to the logic of it, I could see how this would have come about. Though the P move on after their job is done, they do not (as Ayah suggested) leave the colonists totally to their own devices. Yeshmani saw to this and the P enhanced his plan with his very own DNA. A colonist was chosen as a carrier of the P memory and technology. This information has been passed down from generation to generation and mostly lay dormant over time, until a crisis or threat called it back into action. My family has been one of the carriers on Vantanahon, which may explain my overactive awe of the P, for I have the memory banks of the P at my fingertips. The same ones I used to massage Durmah's neck earlier.

Durmah

Rander went off and Ayah moved to follow, but Lucrea motioned him to stay put and she left to be with him. I decided to break the tension by telling everyone of this bizarre dream I had, coincidentally set on the Mother Planet, home of Yeshmani and the origins of the P. There were large mammals living in the seas called whales. We have dolphins in the seas here, but none of these large leviathans. They were, intelligent and mostly peaceful. Unfortunately, they were hunted mostly to extinction because of the profit that could be made from selling products made from their bodies. It is so difficult for us to understand that this killer mentality was so much apart of the survival history of the First Ones that we forget that is used to be part of ours as well. Their history is our history.

"In this dream, I am swimming with the whales and they are singing this haunting song which sounds like whistles and horns. These creatures are the size of houses and yet so gentle and spiritual..." here I got choked up and shed a tear, much to my embarrassment.

'Already I can see him opening and being less full of himself,' smirked Ayah, glad that Durmah had managed to soften the tone caused by Rander's reaction to the details of their mission. He looked on the deck in the partial sunset time of the one sun setting after the other. Lucrea had her hand on Rander's shoulder and then stepped back and gasped.

'So, now she knows.' sighed Ayah as he turned back to the fire. 'Everyone will know soon. I wonder who's the best person to fill them in on this little development?'

Lucrea

I stopped Ayah from going after my brother and followed Rander out of the warm, smelly room. We had always had a special bond and I knew his feelings about the P, how he had come to worship them. They had always been a mystery in my family, it seemed, more than the others. My mother especially seemed to have some connection with them that she imparted on to Rander, somehow. The rest of us just assumed it was something in their inner natures, a common chord that rang when the P were brought up. I'd respected it and never asked about it, until now. Something I saw in Rander's eyes as he stormed out told me that there was more to the story and that I may not like the details, bedeviled as they can get. "Rander" I said as I put my hand on his shoulder. Without turning around, he stared straight ahead into the sunset and said simply, as a matter of factly, "I am the Parushaha."

I gasped and stood back, my hand tingling. "How do you mean?"

"They are in me, a part of me. They have been transferred down, though our family from the time of the first landing. It was part of Yeshmani's plan to make sure the colonists had access to the P's memory in times of need or crisis. Then, one of us in each generation is called to come forward and assist.

"Why didn't I know?! Why wasn't I told? Do we all have them inside?" I shivered at the thought of sharing my body with a machine.

"Just one of us, and we never know who...until around the age of 10 when the first signs of their presence are seen by the one who passed them on to us...mom. Until then, mom knew they could be realized in any one of us."

"So mom knew..." I said quietly.

"They came from mom just as they will come from me. Of course, it will be more interesting since I'm Sumitrahn. In my case, I can choose who will receive the gift, if you can call it that."

I didn't know whether to be relieved or upset that Rander was the host of the P and not me. Was this one more thing to make him special and me just run-of-the-mill? I was just amazed that my mother was able to keep the secret for so long. After I was able to work my own personal ego out of the equation, I thought to ask, "What's it like, to have them as a part of you?"

"Mostly I forget they are in me," Rander began thoughtfully. "I know of their presence and have learned to take care not to activate them unless they're needed." Rander blushed.

"What is it?" asked Lucrea.

"When I masturbate, I have to make sure they aren't released with the ejaculate. I can control that, and in me, it's how they can be transferred to the next one."

"So mother told you about them at puberty, before the Jinbatan?" I remembered being surprised that it was she who talked to him before the Coming of Age Ceremony and not my father or uncles. I'd assumed it was because he was Sumitahn, that his partners would be male and not female or not flexible, as is the case with me. I'm Hanahan.

"Yes, and you can imagine how awkward that was. Mother telling me what I must and must not think and do when I get off!"

We both laughed and rejoined the group just as Ayah was about to tell them about Rander's little secret.

Rander

I hear Ayah saying, "There's something you all should know," and move to stop him.

"No Ayah, let me tell them. It is my duty." I interrupted just as he finished his sentence. He nodded and sat down near the fire watching me keenly; was that respect on his brow? I hoped so. I'd been childish long enough in my life.

"The thing you all should know, that Ayah knows, and now Lucrea," and she stood by me holding on to my arm as I said this, thankful of her support, "is that I carry the knowledge of the P within me."

"How's that possible?!" exclaimed Durmah.

"And why you?" added Ede, immediately embarrassed at the thought of how that might have sounded.

I explained as best I could and answered their questions. Lucrea talked about her surprise at just finding out and Ayah and Sen, as my lovers, told the group that I was under an obligation (which I only found out about at my Jinbatan) to tell all my partners about the P I carry inside me. Each partner is a potential host, if I deem they are the ones to receive my 'gift.'

"Some gift," quipped Durmah and I could tell what he was thinking, since I'd sensed he'd always desired me, but it had never came to pass. I met his eyes and he looked away quickly into the fire.

The Mission

"So let me tell you how we plan to use our access to the P through Rander to try to restabilize the vortex at Indrasiah." Ayah and Rander stood in front of the fire, facing the group.

"It's simple really," continued Rander. "Once we arrive at the vortex and assess the situation, with Ede and Durmah's expertise, I will activate the P and together we'll analyze the data and hopefully come up with a plan of action."

"Have you activated them before? What does it feel like?" Lucrea's question was on everyone's mind.

"Only once, after the Jinbatan, when I had to do a dry run, or a wet run as it turned out. I remember going into a trance and Sen was there to help me, (ever confident, he merely smirked rather than looking away or turning red) when I came, so did they and it was like a hologram, image after image, welcoming me and telling me how they could be accessed and when, there were only two occasions allowed: when the knowledge is needed in a time of crisis or emergency and second, the time of transferal.

Since I am Sumitahn, and not Mahantahn, or even Hanahan, I can choose the one to whom I do the transfer. My mother, being Mahantahn, knew the P inside her would be transferred to one of her children, but did not know which one it would be.

"So Sen is here since he was there the first time and knows the process. Ayah, as my current lover, will do the activation. Durmah and Edie will need to help us decipher the information and integrate it into what we already know about the vortex and Indrasiah and last, but not least, Lucrea is our medicine woman and food procurer. Without her skills, we could not get there or manage the return."

'And me,' I thought to myself, 'I'm the key.'

"Here I thought this was some sort of Svatsia that we as healers and academes were all going on together," mentioned Ede, with some disappointment.

"It is that, in a way," Ayah added putting his hand on Ede's wild mane. "Except the goal is not personal enlightenment for healing, it is planetary healing that we are after."

"Do we have any idea as to how or even if we can pull this off?" Durmah, always the skeptic.

"The Modals are all enlisted," quipped Ayah, the Grammarian, "Have to and the stronger must (or is it the other way around?), ought to, should, can, may, might not, could possibly, but in the end, the bottom line, had better or else!"

"And we'll know more once we get there and the P are enlisted." Rander mused.

"We're in the army now," sighed Ede and got up to go to her bed. The others followed.

Well, not immediately, and not all of them. Ayah and Rander went to try out the hot springs and Lucrea went for a walk down by the lake. Durmah followed Ede to her bed and lingered, "You in the mood for me, Ede?"

"I'm always in the mood for you, Durmah, " she purred, "And especially tonight with all this," She gestured to the surroundings, "going on. Come give me one of your famous Rhetiormayan treatments and we'll see where that leads us."

Rhetiorma is a form of energy healing taught to everyone, men and women, during their Ka Jinbatan. The Master of Rhetiorma could channel the universal energy force through the recipient's body, aligning and balancing all the rapha, or energy points of the body. It was an old skill that had been lost and rediscovered time immemorial, dating back to the First Ones on the Home Planet. It was the same universe, though, no matter how many galaxies removed they were from those First Ones, and the same energy flowing through bodies not so different from the originals. There had been adjustments, improvements, the occasional P factor, but mostly the initial design had withstood the test of time and the fine tuning of it had become an art.

Senthion

I sat alone by the fire, feeling like I'd hoped I wouldn't...left out. I'd prepared myself for Rander going off with Ayah, hand in hand, and though I knew I could have joined them, and would have been welcomed, there was the Ka Daklu they had done and I didn't quite feel like it. I'd also seen Durmah follow Ede and Lucrea go off by herself, which left me to my thoughts.

I regretted now that I didn't bring Ashtu, my meerkat, along. She would have loved the adventure and getting out. More importantly, she could provide the company I'll need with the dynamics of this particular group of travelers. Everyone loved Ashtu, especially Lucrea, with whom I'd be sharing my sleeping compartment. Jumping up, I realized a decision had just been made; I could use the body transfer to get Ashtu and be back before anyone knew I was gone. I always slept better with her curled up on my chest, so as I closed my eyes and was gone in an instant, I looked forward to seeing my companion's surprise as I appeared before her to bring her along on the mission. "Every mission deserves its animal muse," I flashed as I reappeared at my friend's house, in the very room Ashtu had claimed as her sleeping area for the night. "I'm here to take you along," I transmitted in thought and Ashtu jumped onto my shoulder.

Ashtu

"Ashtu's here!" announced Lucrea at breakfast and everyone looked up in surprise.

"I thought Sen decided not to bring her and in fact, she didn't come out with us..." Durmah stated and then stopped.

"I just saw her sleeping on his chest when I woke up," added Lucrea cheerfully. "It looks like Sen changed his mind about her coming along..."

Rander looked confused, "I didn't know you could teach body transfer to animals," and then he eyed Ayah who had not yet taught it to him scornfully.

"I think he must have gone and got her," smirked Ayah, "unless there are ways I do not yet know...which is always possible and makes this existence more interesting..."

"I thought body transfer was almost a sacred ritual and not to be used lightly, as in fetching something you forgot..." Durmah's conservative streak. "I was under the impression that on a mission such as ours, we needed to go on foot, the traditional way, with no assistance from you Sensitive types."

"Ayah uses it playfully to catch me off guard," Rander put in, "and I don't see any issue with Sen making himself more comfortable."

"I just don't like the idea of an animal along on a mission. It doesn't feel proper." Durmah's' world view clouded over the otherwise cheerful breakfast table.

"Shh. They're awake" cautioned Ayah. Everyone stared silently at the now cold fire's ashes as each contemplated the import of this new development.

'Who would have thought it'd be Sen and indirectly Ashtu who'd cause the first schism in the group?' pondered Ayah to himself. 'The dynamics of any group are never predictable.'

'Damn that Durmah,' thought Rander. 'He has no right to judge Sen and his inclusion of Ashtu on this mission. Who is he of value to anyway? Lucrea or Ede could easily do what he is supposed to do. Vaya! I thought I was the conservative one with my feelings about the P...'

Ede eyed Durmah who was stewing in his heating juices. 'So gentle in bed and yet so hard and stubborn in life. Where is that tenderness I experienced last night?'

Lucrea was the most appalled at all that had just transpired. She loved everyone in the room and had a special feeling for Ashtu and the relationship she had developed with Sen. She wished she had an animal spirit to bring along. 'I'll have to ask Sen about that...'

Lastly, Durmah fumed to himself, 'Damn Sensitives and their animals. Other species relationships should not be allowed by the rules of the Budhaun.'

The Budhaun

When the colonists are first seeded on a new planet, they are not only left with access to the P, but also a set of rules developed and refined over the ages. On Vantanahon, this is called The Budhaun. The secret to the B's longevity is in its flexibility. As a particular people evolve, rules need to be changed or fine-tuned and there's always an element, reflected in Durmah's behavior, which clings to the old rules...or dreams of more rules to counter behavior they don't approve of. It is no easy matter, however, to change The Budhaun. Any change requires the consensus of the current population and that occurs only after rounds of endless meetings with long, drawn-out discussions often segueing off onto tangents inspired by personal preferences and individual differences. There was now a growing faction favoring restrictions on species interaction, so Durmah was not alone in his opinions. In these stressful times of planetary flux, people were looking for scapegoats and a conservative vein was swelling in the planets human body and its pulse could be felt in discussions and political debate. In addition, the younger generation seen in Rander was turning out conservative as well. Therefore, it was a sign of the times that at least one member of the mission should question the use of body transfer and another have an issue with Ashtu coming along.

The most recent change in The Budhaun was the demystification of body transfer. Confusion still existed about the status of this process, evinced by Durmah's' older interpretation, long since altered these 100 moons, and more tellingly, Rander's confusion. He was in line to succeed Ayah after he'd mastered all the teachings, most importantly that of body transfer itself. Ayah was one of the 12 planetary representatives on the Budhaun's council. He represented the Healer. Also represented on the council were The Hanahan, The Sumitahn, The Mahantahn, The Parushaha, The Grower, The Harvester, The Midwife, The Thinker, The Sensitive, The Historian and The Jayhvasu or Leader. The Leader is always mentioned last because he or she has the least importance on the B...mostly a figurehead, or even sometimes referred to as The Necessary Evil. S/he is a facilitator most of the time, ever since the time of conflict ended and The Budhaun replaced other laws or creeds. There used to be the position of The Protector, but as The Budhaun evolved, such a role had been replaced by the Sensitive. Protection was no longer required after the people had grown out of their aggressive tendencies.

Though evolution is slow, it is sure and clearly the Budhaun has evolved along with the people over time. The original B sent out with the First P by Yeshmani is quite a different set of rules than the ones currently known to Ayah and his companions.

The Original 10 Budhaun Rules

Yeshmani had had plenty of time to come up with the rules he would include in the very first Budhaun that he carried with him personally as he boarded the ship that would take him and the still developing P onto its interception with the comet, Shanta.

He had the home planet's rules as a base and his own ethics as building blocks for the new set. He decided on ten, not any more, no less. Even during his time, long before the wheels of greed set in motion years before had begun the destruction of the planet, Yeshmani could see what was going wrong and had some ideas on how to prevent this on future worlds. People had lost the respect for the planet they lived on that the Ancients had had. They were using up its resources faster than ever before and this trend would only get worse.

Rule One, therefore, had to address respect for the planet to be seeded with colonists. Life could not be destroyed, only enhanced. The terraforming could not damage existing life forms and the colonists must adapt and fit into their new environment. There were endless debates on contamination and past mistakes were studied and avoided at all costs. Fortunately, the universe is a big place and life in it, from sentient to microbial, is a rare occurrence. Many planets were passed up by adhering strictly to the first rule of the Budhaun: Peaceful Coexistence. The impartial mechanic nature of the P enabled this adherence to continue, unabated by more human flexibility. Life and resources would never again be sacrificed at the altar of Greed. Ironically it would be this first rule, broken through ignorance and neglect that would again cause problems on Vantanahon.

Rule Two, Diversity, had to do with the make up of the original colonists. There needed to be equality, equal distribution of both gender and sexual orientation, race and philosophy. They all needed to be volunteers, and so the actual original number varied form planet to planet. Rule Three involved Self-Governance. At least at first, organization was key and a strong leader would be more important than in subsequent times. As you can see, these first three rules would be the first to be changed as the society evolved and moved on from the beginning stages of initial settlement.

The consensus model, though at times unwieldy, was chosen as the method of decision making, meaning 100% agreement was needed from the group and any one person could block consensus if s/he felt that the decision was counter to the good of the group as a whole. Rules Four through Seven were practical considerations which dealt with the division of labor required to establish the society on a planet. There were the Healers, the Growers and the Harvesters and the Thinkers. From birth, one was assigned to a group based on the intuition of the Midwife assisting the birth. The Thinkers would plan the living and growing spaces and put the Growers to work as soon as possible. The Harvesters would assist in the building and maintenance of the areas until Harvest time, when the Growers whose work was done for that year, would take over for them. While they reaped what they had sown, the Healers, who originally included the Midwives and the Sensitives, would take care of everyone, using local remedies whenever possible, but relying at first on the pharmacy left behind by the P with the first set of provisions.

The Eighth rule addressed the issue of Self-sufficiency. This was to be attained as soon as possible as the P could only stay and assist for a limited period of time replicating the supplies needed by the new settlements. The sooner the planet became self-sufficient, the faster the P could move on to the next Seeding. This process usually took five years, a short time in the Eternal Lives of the Parushaha...an eternity at times for the colonists. Rule Nine had to do with Vegetarianism. Only plants were brought in the form of seeds and seedlings, for food, no animals came from the home planet or subsequent colonies. The only animals brought were the companions of the original settlers, birds, cats, dogs, pigs, meerkats and ferrets. Small creatures which would be easy to transport were required to be treated equally and never to be used as food. Not all colonists had them, but the rule of Vegetarianism nevertheless stood for all planets, a few of which maintained their own life forms, which could possibly be used as food in an emergency, but as a result of Rule Nine, never were. Finally Rule Ten had to do with Spirituality. Each colonist was allowed to follow whatever path to Spiritual Enlightenment s/he felt best suited to his/her temperament. However, sometimes the planet itself offered its own form of Spirituality.

Vantanahon Spirituality

The Spirit of the planet Vantanahon was particularly strong. Even the P, essentially non-spiritual beings, felt this as part of their original probing. Because of the nearness of the two suns and the timing of the risings and settings, the colonists could live above ground on Vantanahon and many species of plants especially trees and bushes, flourished. Vantanahon already had its own life which developed quickly with the enriching of the atmosphere with carbon and oxygen. Silicon-based life forms were able to co-exist with the carbon-based settlers and the plants and animals they brought with them. Over time, hybrids of the two life forms developed. It was in these hybrids that the Spirituality unique to the planet developed and influenced the colonists to a great degree. They loved their new home and the planet nourished them.

This nourishing power, concentrated in vortexes distributed around the planet, became places of worship and healing, the greatest being Indrasiah, where the group was now heading. The P were well aware of these vortexes, but did not probe deeply enough to see how their development would/could affect the overall health of the planet and the colonists. An imbalance of energy was causing a breach and the energy was no longer contained. It had begun to escape into space, first at the Indrasiah vortex and soon at the others. Once the energy was released into space, it dissipated and was lost to the planet and its inhabitants.

Journey to Indrasiah

"Durmah thinks that you shouldn't have brought Ashtu on the mission," Lucrea blurted as Sen came in to breakfast. Sen and Ashtu joined the now silent breakfast group and ignored the tension in the room. Ashtu sat on Sen's shoulder as he fed her grapes and balls of melon from his plate. He chatted blithely of his dreams and even asked Durmah to get them some cereal from the kitchen. When he was out of the room, Sen asked calmly, "Is there any other opposition to Ashtu's coming along?" Everyone shook their heads in the negative.

"Then, I'll deal with Durmah on the road. Leave him to us." Ashtu jumped down and sat in Durmah's' chair just as he returned. He put the cereal down in front of Sen and looking at his now occupied chair, took a seat across the table.

"Durmah probably thinks that it was inappropriate for me to use the body transfer to get her as well," added Sen blandly as he dished up fruit onto the cereal grains. "Durmah thinks too much and too narrowly. That has been my observation." Sen sat down across from Durmah and stared into his eyes. Durmah reddened again and looked down.

"Play nice, you two," cautioned Ayah, "we haven't even stepped on the trail yet. I personally see no problem with Ashtu joining us. To be fair though, we could get a consensus..."

Durmah got up and left the room saying, "I'll meet you all out front in an hour. I won't block consensus over an animal."

Lucrea gave Ashtu some cereal in a bowl and watched her eat. Sen sighed and ate the rest of his fruit. The others got up one by one to go to their rooms and pack. Rander came to sit by Sen.

"Are you up to this? Sorry he's being a pain. You know, we could have kept you company at night."

"It is not the work I'd planned to be doing at this point in the mission, but it's important work to be done, nevertheless. The more minds we can turn to our cause...here he nodded to Ashtu, the better. Yes, I know I would have been welcome with you two, but Ashtu is my choice of companion these days." Sen's eyes shone with devotion and determination.

They were all finally gathered in front of the lodge, ready to go. Sen and Ashtu had already started, gone up ahead as part of Sen's plan with Durmah. Ayah and Rander stood waiting for the others. Durmah came out with Ede and Lucrea hitched up her skirts and started after Sen and Ashtu.

"How she can hike in those skirts, I'll never figure out," Ede was trimmed down and svelte in her tight jumpsuit toped with a flowing cloak. Durmah looked almost her twin except for the darker colors and the boots on his feet. "I have to admit that she is light on her feet and never seems to tire..."

"in spite of her girth," Durmah completed. "I see some of the party has already taken off. Are we foregoing the ritual send-off?" It was obvious that Durmah was not going to let this perceived slackness in observing the rules of a mission go quietly.

"The first sun is not quite up yet, Durmah. We'll meet up ahead and combine the inspiration with the send-off..." Ayah explained patiently.

"Just want to be kept in the loop," started Durmah with his rugged hands splayed out in front of him, "I don't think it's wise to start out by cutting corners..."

"Enough with the..." started Rander irritably.

"Rander." interrupted Ayah, "Let me." Which seemed to infuriate Durmah even more, opposite to the intended placation.

"Let him have his say. I won't have smoldering resentment on my mission." Huffed Durmah, busying himself with his packs.

"You should have thought of that when you initiated the whole hoopla over Ashtu. So unnecessary, yet so like you: The center of the universe. And by the way, who died and made you Yeshmani of this particular mission. Last I heard, it was 'our' mission."

Ayah saw the sense in letting these two have it out, so he took Ede's arm and they followed Lucrea down the road to catch up with Sen and Ashtu.

"Good idea," inserted Ede, her cloak flapping in the early morning breeze. The first sun was just rising in the north. "Sometimes I just don't understand Durmah. How does one get to be so closed?"

"Life experience, what he has learned up till now has colored how he sees us and how he feels we should all interact," explained Ayah, his expressive hands tossing shadows onto the gravel path.

"It is dangerous, is it not, this limited view of his?" Ede was adjusting her pack to best fit her frame, making accommodations for her full bosom and her tiny waist. Durmah had offered to take part of her allotted load, but she'd refused. 'I can carry my own weight,' she had bristled, yet feeling the caring and tender concern behind his offer. This contradiction caused her no end of confusion, especially since Durmah planned to share her bed along the way and she had no desire to prevent that from happening.

"Very," Ayah's brow wrinkled uncharacteristically. "I'm just hoping Sen's plan will work with him. Otherwise, we may not have the total combined force to accomplish our mission." They walked the rest of the way in silence.

Rander and Durmah

"Walk with me?" Rander asked politely and he took Durmah's arm. Durmah fell in comfortably beside him and Rander thanked the stars above that orientation was not one of Durmah's issues. He'd read tales of old that told of earlier times when men like Durmah would not be caught dead with men like Rander. It seemed so strange, considering the present reality of all three sexual orientations considered important enough to deserve a seat each on the Budhaun Council. Considering how differently each orientation saw the world, no wonder that old society, now long dead, but not forgotten thanks to the Historians and what they kept in the Archives, was always at odds with itself and as a result at war with its many factions. The men like Durmah, the Mahantahn, were mostly in charge, from time to time, one of the women. A recipe for disaster! Once in a rare while, a Hanahan would be in control and even more rarely, a Sumitahn like Rander...for they were often shunned and had to live secret lives, passing for Mahantahn. 'As if...' Rander tried to imagine pulling such a thing off. "Truly a skill in acting," he found himself saying out loud.

"What's a skill in acting?" asked Durmah.

"A Sumitahn trying to pass for a Mahantahn."

"Why would anyone try to do that?" he wondered innocently and Rander suddenly saw his distance from Durmah decreasing.

Sen & the Others, Minus Rander and Durmah

First Lucrea caught up with Sen and Ashtu leapt from Sen's shoulder to hers. "No problems with acceptance here, I see," winked Sen as he watched Ashtu snuggle up on Lucrea's neck.

"Maybe she smells a bit of Rander on me..." Lucrea pondered. "I often wondered if he were part of the attraction Ashtu seems to have for me."

"She did quite like Rander, but don't underestimate yourself, Lucrea. Meerkats are more sensitive than Sensitives when it comes to friend or foe...all animals are. Sometimes I think that's why men, Mahantahn men especially, sometimes fear them, as we fear the Truth. Funny how it's only men we have to worry about. Rarely do women have this problem."

"Maybe it comes from ancestral memories. It was the Mahantahn men who traditionally hunted animals for food in the days before the Seedings."

"Residual memories sparking long dormant hormones triggering long unused responses. Interesting Lucrea. I don't know. I'd prefer to think it's more an individual fault. Like being too overbearing or arrogant, both of which we see in Durmah, by the way."

"You won't get far with him with your mind on that track, Sen."

"I know, I know. Give me time to work it through."

They were cresting a hill and looked back to see the trees in which the lodge stood, the unusual sight of smoke coming up. Over there was the pond Ayah liked to calm himself by and ahead, the trail that lead in the direction of Indrasiah, Departieh, Naha and Rapha. Everywhere was green or grayish green, the colors of old Mahavat, the First Place, home of the First Ones, Yeshmani and the origins of the technology which brought everyone everywhere. Thanks to the Parushaha. Here and there, the silicon-carbon hybrids, the colors of Vantanahon interspersing, blues with the greens and grays, white trunks, black branches, their leaves, if they fall, dissolve rather than dry up. No flowers on Vantanahon, only trees, bushes and grasses. Even the fruit did not flower, it appeared in miniature form, like figs or dates, old species adapted to space travel and adapting to a variety of conditions on a multitude of worlds. The sky was turning its own Vantanahan color of yellow and orange as the second sun began its ascent into the sky. The colors on this world were in the sky, not on the ground.

Morning Rituals

They all stood and took in the morning ceremony of re-light, after the hours of darkness with two suns; the absence of both was particularly felt by Vantanahans. Over the years, the populace had developed several morning rituals to celebrate this unique time.

As a rule, people rose before the Risings and prepared themselves for the day. Cleanings and feedings took place so everyone could be outside to be with the first and then second rising. They'd face Schmanaha, the first sun, and feel its warmth on their faces as it rose. They'd empty their thoughts and be open for the inspiration. Tradition held that the sun had a special message for each person on the planet, directing him or her on the best path for that day. Sometimes, it was a vague inkling, finish that project or start a new one, but other times, it was astonishingly clear. Go here at this time and do this and leave at that time, having accomplished the pre-ordained task. Eyes open at the Deshmaha's rising, the people would do their breathing and stretching exercises, the Gayo, and set off to their work or play.

So on this, the first Rising of the first day of their mission, there was much anticipation for what inspiration Schmanaha and Deshmaha would bring each of them, including Ashtu.

Inspiration

Sen was the first to receive something. His eyes closed, mind cleared, he had a clear image of him walking with Durmah, with Ashtu sitting happily on Durmah's shoulder. The look in Durmah's eyes showed the extent of his conversion. With stunned recognition, Sen realized the look in Ashtu's eyes meant she was Durmah's now. "Am I prepared to give up Ashtu to Durmah?" Sen asked himself. "Is this the price I have to pay for a peaceful mission? And how could that even be possible?"

Ashtu saw it too, and it confused her meerkat logic. Sitting on the enemy's shoulder, looking that satisfied, belonging to him... how can these things be?

Ayah felt a sober awareness seep into his consciousness as the sun leaked behind his eyelids. He dared not, at first, hazard a guess as to what all the bright light meant, images of their part of the galaxy, other galaxies, the Home Galaxy...Could that be what Mahavat looked like, before it was destroyed by its greedy populace? It seemed so familiar, yet so utterly foreign. This was the stuff that the ancients referred to as 'heavenly.' He recalled from Vantanahon tradition that when one died, he or she would experience in the afterlife his or her own concept of what it would be to be in heaven. Ayah had always imagined his soul traveling the universe, like the P, eternally when he died. Now to see his version of heaven seemed like a version of hell. He'd heard about this kind of inspiration - a portent of imminent death—were these things that had to be?

Lucrea saw her role in Durmah's reconciliation with Ashtu. It could not be accomplished by Sen alone, and Ashtu had a role, too. She too saw Ashtu on Durmah's shoulder, being his animal companion.

Ede waited patiently for something to come to her. She saw the others receive theirs, she could tell by their faces. She'd peeked, opened her eyes to slits though it was officially not allowed. She saw Sen's confusion, Ayah's disbelief, Lucrea's determination. She had nothing. It had been like this lately, no inspiration with Schmanaha's rising, no little images as clear as day...nothing. It usually meant, for women, that they were with child, but that could not be possible, she thought even as she felt Durmah still inside her.

Back on the path, Rander and Durmah were stopped to face the sun. Rander immediately saw the P within him as soon as he closed his eyes to welcome the first sun. What happened next was not expected. He'd expected the P to be part of his inspiration this morning, but he would never have thought how much like the P he'd become after they were accessed. He barely recognized himself as he saw himself standing alone with swirling clouds at his feet.

'Why alone?' He asked himself. 'Where was Ayah? And the others?'

Durmah hadn't known what to expect. He'd had clear inspirations before but this time, he wondered what would come to him.

Sometimes the duty is hard and the timing is bad, but the universe, the Jesicaahn, can not be denied. In these cases, when your life can be turned around in a day, you see only flowers as your inspiration. Flowers are Legend on Vantanahon because they did not get seeded there – it was a planet of greens, grays and blues – but no bright colors. The reds, oranges, yellows could only be seen in the sky. You need to look up to see such wonders. They are not scattered all around so that you could rightly step on them if you weren't paying attention – like on other worlds or as it was on the Home Planet. So, when Jesicaahn fills your inspiration with the vivid and strange forms of flowers, you know you're in for it. Something life changing is about to happen and that's exactly what Durmah saw as he closed his eyes on this first morning of what he thought was an ill-fated mission. He almost laughed in his wonderment. He'd never seen flowers. He'd heard of them and seen artist renderings in the Archives, but nothing could have prepared him for the real thing. All shapes, color combinations, complete with fragrance, another detail left out of

Vantanahon's schemata, filled his head as he realized what had come to him on this day.

It is customary to share your inspiration for the day. After the rising of the second sun, Deshmaha, the seven travelers gather on the top of the rise. Their way stretched out in front of them, disappearing into the foothills of the Kaymah.

"I might as well go first," started Ede looking frustrated and a bit downcast. "I got nothing. It's happened before, but to get nothing today is doubly annoying." Durmah, who's had the most radical inspiration, shocking even compared to Ayahs' premonition of his own death, wanted to chime in after Ede, that he'd seen nothing either, but the image of flowers was too compelling not to share, so he simply said,

"I saw flowers."

After the audible gasp from Rander, Sen murmured, "Well that makes my work a lot easier," which got a smile even out of Durmah, "and my inspiration a little clearer, so still not that much easier to take." He then told the others what he had seen.

"I am to help Sen with his reconciliation of Durmah to Ashtu," Lucrea said, taking Sen's hand.

"I saw the P and how they will change me, but I was all alone." Rander looked to Ayah.

"Nothing for me." Was Ayah's only reply, which caused Rander to emit his second gasp of the day. Sen eyed Ayah suspiciously, knowing that was a veiled comment and his eyes widened as the veil lifted.

They all walked in silence the rest of the morning, until it was time to stop, rest and eat something. Sen and Ashtu sat with Lucrea and Ede, eating the travel food the lodge had packed for them – hard, nutritious cakes of fruit and nuts which kept forever and filled you up quickly. Rander and Durmah were standing together as Ayah went off to scout up ahead.

"I'm going to him," and Rander was off, leaving Durmah uncomfortably alone with his newly found 'flower power'.

"And I'm going to him," Sen announced as Ashtu jumped to Lucrea's lap and he started over to where Durmah was sitting.

"So, flowers, eh? Tell me, I've never seen them in an inspiration – it is truly special."

"It is; I can't describe them in words." Durmah reached out and took Sen's hand and clasped it, allowing the emotions and images of the flowers to be transferred – to Sen's consciousness.

"Oh," he breathed in suddenly, overwhelmed by Durmah's gift and the images of the flowers. Durmah held Sen's hand until the images stopped and Sen opened his eyes.

"How can I thank you? What possessed you to share with me so completely?"

"It's hard to explain," Durmah started softly. "Ever since the images appeared to me, my mind is prompting me to do things totally out of my character."

"I've heard that the flowers can do that." Sen was thoughtful, a tear in his eye. "Will you share these images with the others?"

"No, only with you." Durmah looked off in the direction of Lucrea and Ashtu and made eye contact with Ashtu for the first time since she had arrived.

Rander found Ayah standing still, looking off into the mountains, which looked so near, yet so far. He walked up to him and stood next to him. 'I wish I could do body transfer...' he thought again, resentful of Ayah's reluctance to teach me so far.

"I might just have to teach you the body transfer technique today." Ayah announced matter-of-factly, as if he had read Rander's thoughts. Had he?

Rander's initial glee was overcome by dread when he added nothing and submission together. "What does this mean?" he asked tentatively not sure he wanted to hear the answer. "Are you going to leave? What about the Ka Daklu? Why was I alone, on high, in the clouds? Am I going to die?" Rander had never thought of this possibility before.

"I saw the Ka Daklu lying in the dust, broken. No dear one, it is not you who's going to die. I am the one who may not be returning from this mission."

Rander was stunned and cut to the bone by Ayah's bluntness. It was so unexpected, this attitude, this inspiration. He didn't quite know how to deal with it. Tears welled up in his green eyes and fell down his cheeks to the path below them.

"Oh Rander," Ayah hugged him close. "I'm so sorry. I didn't know how else to tell you. I knew it'd hurt, imagine how I feel! At first, I didn't want to tell anyone-I was in denial. Then, I withdrew into myself. I grew cold and detached. I just wanted to say what I saw, what I felt. I should have been thinking of you and the others. It is you all who will be left behind. I'll be set free, sooner than I'd imagined, to roam this universe at my will."

"This isn't making me feel any better," sobbed Rander as he clung to Ayah, and then pushed him away violently. "How can this be happening to us now, so soon after the Ka Daklu? Is Jesicaahn that cruel?"

"Jesicaahn is Jesicaahn – neither kind nor cruel. I don't comprehend it any more than you do."

"I want you now," and his lips were on Ayah's mouth, intensely, desperately trying to taste him deeply, to make it last, to try to stop his memory from fading once he's gone, as he knew it would.

Durmah saw Ashtu as she was for the first time. He was amazed at the difference. Where once was a dumb animal, dirty even, now he saw a creature of light and wonder that the likes of Sen and Lucrea saw without the aid of a flower transformation.

Ashtu saw that Durmah was seeing her as she was for the first time. 'So that's why, he didn't really see me.' She thought and then turned her attention back to Lucrea.

Just then, Ayah led a weeping, ravaged Rander back into the clearing. Lucrea and Ashtu stood up and went to him. "What happened?" she asked Ayah with concern in her voice.

"I think you all should sit down." began Ayah soberly. "I was being cryptic when I said I had nothing from the inspiration. I was trying to postpone the inevitable, but with so many Sensitives around, that subterfuge just doesn't work. What I meant to say is that I may not be returning form this mission. I don't know when or how, but I saw the light and the star travel and I know enough of my own version of where I want my soul to travel to know my own death when I see it. Rander and I have been trying to come to grips with what this means for us.

There was nothing left to say for the moment, so Ayah picked up his pack and with Rander at his side, they started down the trail. Everyone still had the mission to try to balance a planet with leaking energy and volatile vortices. The others followed them in silence. No one had even thought of death as a part of this task and everyone assumed they'd all come back pretty much as before. Ayah's inspiration pointedly burst all their bubbles.

Ayah turned to Rander, "We really lead sheltered lives as residents of Vantanahon. There is little exposure to death or danger with disease a word in the history books, most people die of old age or in rare occasions, by their own hand. Suicide is not forbidden under the Budhaun, but with depression conquered, or at least managed, and life so painless and easy, it would be a rare path for one to take. Another cause of death is the occasional storms, the Shitsmayeh, that an unlucky soul could get caught in. This is why these recent deaths at Indrasiah caused by the energy imbalance are of great concern. This is why the mission was sponsored by the Budhaun."

Rander, who in his young life had spent precious little time wondering about his mortality, suddenly was confronted with his partner's possible parting. He just stood in stunned silence and reverie, looking at Ayah through tearful eyes.

"When will it happen?" Ede asked Sen and Sen only shook his head. "We are not shown the gory details," he explained, "Only the pleasant aftermath...in Ayah's case, the light and the journey to the stars. Otherwise it'd be too freaky, living up to that final moment you would have seen coming."

"We know it's coming though," countered Ede. "That's freaky enough for me."

"It's always coming Ede," reminded Sen gently.

Durmah was walking with Lucrea and Ashtu, the two former antagonists keeping their distance, yet growing more curious about one another.

"Does it understand what's going on right now?" Durmah was trying to be polite.

"IT is a SHE. 'Does SHE understand?', Durmah. That's the first thing you can do...use the right pronoun with Ashtu."

"OK then, SHE...so she does understand pronouns at least? What else does she understand and how do you know that she does?"

Lucrea smiled. He was trying, in his stilted way. "It's easier with the Sensitives. They can read each other's thoughts. She is as surprised as we are to imagine someone's death ahead of the actual occurrence. She's having trouble with the idea of knowing what the future will bring. She lives mostly in the present."

"Smart girl. I don't much like this kind of knowing ahead of time. I have a hard time believing it can't be prevented. I myself will do my best to watch over Ayah and see what I can do to stop this from happening. We can't lose him."

"Durmah, did you ever stop your thoughts of being our protector long enough to realize that that may be his fate?"

"No. I could never do that. That's why I'm so in demand!"

They fell into a rhythm for the rest of the day, stopping to rest and refuel. As the afternoon wore on, the day lost some of its brilliance and Durmah and Lucrea began scouting for a place to make camp to spend the night. As Schmanaha lowered in its position in the south everyone thought of their inspirations of that day. Though the length of the Vantanahon days were roughly the same as the mother world's, one sun rose in the north and set in the south. The other rose in the west and set in the east. Ede wondered if the next sun would give her any more on what her role in the mission would be.

Senthion's disappearance

"Where's Sen?" Lucrea had noticed Ashtu's agitation and looked around to see that Senthion was not to be seen.

"He'd fallen behind, and I assumed he wanted some time alone," offered Ayah, with Rander looking at him thoughtfully.

"I'll go look for him," Ede was the best tracker amongst them, even better than Durmah, the self-proclaimed scout expert.

"I'll go with you," Rander stepped forward. "I could use the distraction."

The two went back along the path and Rander opened his mind to catch any thoughts that Sen might be sending out. Meanwhile, Ede, not a Sensitive, checked the ground and path.

She recognized everyone's footprints and noticed the absence of Sen's. She heard a noise and turned to see Ashtu in the path.

"Welcome little one." She said, "I can use your skills as well." She smirked at Rander and he realized that Ede did not fully comprehend the extent of Ashtu's "skills", as she referred to them. 'She may be in for a surprise,' he thought to himself.

Ede and Ashtu headed back on the trail until Ede noticed Sen's prints appearing once again. "Which way?" She directed this to Ashtu, as if it were a test. Ashtu did not hesitate and took off to the right, over rocks where no prints would hold. "Scent," she realized and followed Ashtu over the rocks and Rander followed behind them. The rocks led down to a stream and they ended there, along with the scent.

"Here's where I take over," Ede was feeling better now that her skills were being called into use in this search for Sen. She peered across the stream and saw a meadow with horsetail growing in bunches. She knew Sen wouldn't be able to resist collecting some horsetail in case of injury and knowing this fact helped her in the choice of direction.

"He went for the horsetail. I know one of his hobbies is medicinal herbs. We need to cross the stream..." and Ashtu leapt onto her shoulder and they waded across.

"She trusts you," observed Rander as they crossed the stream and headed towards the meadow.

"She has no reason not to," replied Ede. "Unlike Durmah, I have no animosity towards her. I haven't that much experience with the meerkat, but I can see their value on a tracking mission... aside from not wanting to get their feet wet!" laughing, they came into the meadow. "There." she pointed and saw the freshly cut stems of some horsetail. "He *was* here. Tell me Rander, you know Sen better than I do. Is it like him to wander off like that?"

Rander thought for a moment. "You're right, it's not. I saw his face after Ayah told us that he...you know."

"You don't have to say it."

"I know Sen. He wouldn't be able to help but think, that after Ayah's passing, I'd be free again..."

"Rander! He still loves you then." Ede's eyes were wide with scandal.

"You know us...we never really let each other go...Ka Daklu or no."

"You are loyal that way. So, do you see anything else around here that might catch his eye, considering his thoughts of the moment?" Ede saw Rander searching the meadow and his thoughts.

"That silicon hybrid over there..." he started, but stopped, "but he really wouldn't be thinking that..."

"Thinking what?" asked Ede, "Come on, any ideas, no matter how far-fetched..."

"It is said to contain a truth-telling essence and a sexual stimulant."

"Let me guess...to find out your true feelings for him and get you to act on them? Isn't' that all a little too soon? Ayah is still with us."

"That's why I said he really couldn't be thinking that...but it's here and it's a possibility." Rander started over to the bush. "Let's see if any of its branches are cut."

"There are footprints here but I don't see any cuttings," Ede was fingering one of the branches. "Maybe he reconsidered. I should take some back, just in case we are in need of some truth-telling..." She winked at Rander.

"Or a little boost in the sex department?" Rander winked back and cut off a small branch and stuffed it in his bag. "It would be like Sen to at least consider it." he mused and he continued to look for other likely candidates in and around the meadow. "Over there! Now that's something he could not possibly pass up!" Rander was running over to the far edge of the meadow, with Ede and Ashtu following closely behind.

"What is it?" asked Ede, but then saw Ashtu heading over to the large tree trunk, that you could have circled ten people around. "Amazing. Is that what I think it is?"

"I've never been in the parts of Vantanahon where they grow!" Rander touched the trunk reverently. "It's a true mother, thousands of years old, from the time of the Seedings...old growth they called it back on Mahavat. Just touch it to feel the energy! Sen could spend hours here communing with this tree."

"So, Sensitive finds an old growth tree, losing track of time, we find Sen, bring him back in time for supper and all ends well.

Why isn't he here?" Ashtu started up the tree and disappeared into the branches far above them.

"Well, there are two possibilities. Either the tree sent him on its own mission, or...?"

"Or?" Ede didn't think she was going to like the second possibility.

"Or the tree subsumed him. Ashtu will be able to tell us if Sen is still Senthion or now part of this tree." They watched silently for her to reappear.

"Subsumed? So the legends are true?"

"I'm afraid so. There have been documented cases. It is always mutual though, the tree can not take in someone against their will. That's what confuses me. Why would Sen allow such radical change at this time, when he's needed."

"Maybe I wasn't feeling needed." This voice came from above, out of the green, and it was Sen's voice. Soon they saw him descending with Ashtu. "Good job, Ede, my plan worked."

"What plan is that?" she asked, somewhat miffed.

"You were feeling left out. I needed to make you see your role here on this mission. You are such a good tracker..."

"I would never have found the tree, Rander knew about that part." Ede was getting over her shock and initial pissed-offedness.

"And you would never have found the meadow without Ashtu," Rander added. "It seems the lesson is to show how we're all valuable and have our special gifts to contribute to the success of our mission."

"So this is how you plan to get to Durmah..." Ede saw the wisdom in it, "showing him that Ashtu has one value he may not have considered, implying others in the process?"

"It is the first step," started Sen. "Now Rander, as for your theories about my need for that branch you have in your bag..."

They returned to camp, smiles all around. The story was Sen had wandered off to get horsetail and fallen under the spell of the old growth and lost track of time. It took all three of them to finally find Sen, with Ede in the lead, Ashtu smelling and Rander's telling of the old growth attraction. Durmah was silent but Sen sensed an inroad had been forged.

'No more wandering off," announced Ayah. "We are getting into territory none of us know, full of wonders and potential dangers and as Ede has proven, we need each and every (and here he looked from Ashtu to Durmah) one of our talents and knowledge to get us through the Kayonah to Indrasiah. Is that understood?"

With no fires allowed, outside of the special dispensation of the lodge, darkness fell soon and completely after Deshmaha's lingering setting. They erected two-person tubular sleeping compartments, collapsible to the size of an arm. Ayah was sleeping with Rander, Ede with Durmah, and Sen, Lucrea and Ashtu sharing the third. No one on Vantanahon slept alone, for their comfort, protection, and mental well-being. Everyone had a sleeping partner. Ashtu later snuck out and snuggled into the high branches of one of the hybrid trees, keeping watch.

The Presence

"Never having experienced a fire before," Ede said as she nestled up to Durmah's strong, smooth body, "I miss its comfort and warmth."

"You have me for that, we have each other..." Durmah pulled her arms around him. "Fire in the wilds is a volatile luxury. Even in its containment at the lodge, I was nervous."

"Oh, but it extended the hours when we could talk and just enjoy relaxing and the end of the day, everyone being together, safe and warm."

"We need our rest for the journey and besides, you're talking, safe and warm here with me."

'Yes." Ede murmured as she felt him fall asleep and she wondered at the differences between them, all of them, actually. She saw the wisdom of Sen's little lesson today but still resented having had to be 'taught' something. She wondered about the next day's inspiration. Would she continue to be blocked, or would she get some insight this time.

Her dreams of the night might also offer some information, but often dreams were more the letting go of fears and the cleaning out of superfluous ideas in the head than any help of the sort she needed right now. On the other hand, she'd prefer to have nothing than the burden Ayah had received.

From Ashtu's perch high above the campers, she looked out over the dark forest, lit up by her excellent night vision. Other animals were up and active and she wanted to see who they were. Some might be curious about the intruders, might come snooping around. She'd need to keep an eye out for them-she felt protective for them-even the one called Durmah. She felt him coming around, being less of a threat. She'd enjoyed the search for Sen earlier. She'd sensed he was not in danger, not lost, but it was a good exercise. Ede was a good tracker and Rander was smart. She could learn from these humans.

She first sensed only a dark presence and her hair went on end. She couldn't see anything, just a bad feeling in her gut. All animal activity ceased around her and this verified that it wasn't her imagination. The next action wasn't so clear. Should she stay put from her vantage point or go down to warn Sen and Lucrea? She was just about to descend when the intruder gave her a shove and she went flying into the night sky. Landing on Ayah and Rander's compartment, just as they were climaxing, causing it as well as the climax to collapse around them all.

"What the...?" shouted Rander, replacing the previous pleasurable moan.

"Something just landed on top of us!!" Ayah concluded, from its size and dead weight, it's ether a large pine cone or a smallish animal. He felt the round ball between them and ruled out pine.

"It's Ashtu!" sensed Rander "and she's unconscious. How ever did she land on our tent?"

Soon, Ayah was holding the still meerkat in his hands, performing Rhetiorma, a form of energy healing. As consciousness returned, he also sensed fear and realized the danger. "She's been attacked. I can feel it."

"Attacked?" Rander felt as if his sheltered world were coming undone. First death, now attack? What's next, plague or pestilence?

"It was something unseen, but not unexpected. She'd been up in the trees on the lookout. The next thing she remembers is falling through the air – down. I better go out and check on the others."

There was a lot of activity in the camp as everyone was emerging from their sleeping compartments to find out what had happened.

Durmah began, "We know now that we *are* being watched. Time will tell if we are being followed as well. Ede, let's scout around and see if we can find anything. Ayah, is Ashtu fit to come along?"

"She's a bit discombobulated, but the Rhetiorma has helped. Why don't you ask her yourself.."

"And how am I supposed to accomplish that? I don't speak meerkat." Sniped Durmah.

"It's simple," interjected Ede. "I did it this afternoon when we were on Sen's little lesson-teaching foray. You just think your request and she'll respond."

"I think I can give it a try," Durmah looked in Ashtu's direction, like he was trying to see through her with his x-ray vision.

Ashtu flinched and then slowly got up and walked in their direction. The three of them took off in the direction Ashtu lead.

Lucrea and Sen helped Rander get their compartment in order Ayah went off in the opposite direction to see what he could see. No one found any traces of the Presence and by the time everyone returned, the morning lights were starting to show themselves in the northeast.

Inspiration Day 2

Ashtu's run-in with the unknown was the pre-rising buzz as people prepared for the second day's inspiration.

"I wish I had been up there with her," Durmah fumed, pacing the grounds as the compartments were collapsed. Individual heating devices were sending the smells of hot morning drinks up into the lightening sky. Oranges, reds and yellows and violets streaked the sky as Schmanaha began its ascent from the underworld. "Vaya! I could have caught whatever it was- found out its purpose."

"I couldn't sense anything when I was out looking," announced Ayah, "and your search team came up with nothing as well. If we're indeed being followed, rather than just being watched in this one place, you'll have another chance to 'catch it' as you put it. We don't even know what it is that we're dealing with."

"Hush you two; it's time," snarled Ede, impatient for a good inspiration this time. Ashtu hissed as Durmah stepped to close to her tail.

"Everyone's on edge today," Sen observed as he turned to the sun. What he saw at first, did not surprise or please him. He would be taking over on the Budhaun after Ayah's passing. He would not be taking over in Rander's heart or bed, however.

He saw them each going in a different way, swirling separately on another plane. Then he saw himself with Ede. Ede and not Rander, but somehow Rander was still involved and now there was a baby and the baby was Ede's and...Rander's? It just didn't make any sense to him.

Ayah had been wondering what his subsequent inspiration after that of his death would be. Where could they take him beyond the point of no return? He'd read that some people see into the next life, some replay old inspirations-comforting reruns of days-gone-by. Still others get the same last inspiration-repetitive repeats of what is to come, day after day, until the last day is reached, ending it all. A rare few just have the peace of no more inspirations-their job done, they can take it easy, slide into eternity quietly.

It was therefore a surprise when his second day inspiration was none of the above. It was a perfectly normal one-like he'd have on any other day of his life. It was a relief and he began to question whether he had interpreted the first day's message correctly. Had he put everyone one through all this grief over a mistaken interpretation? For the first time in a rising, he began to feel hope, like it wasn't all finished – that his life wasn't over. Should he tell the others? At least Rander should know; he has a right to know, what with the Ka Daklu...what if positions were reversed? He would want to know there was a shadow of a doubt, something to look forward to...

Rander picked up where he left off at his last inspiration – high up in the clouds, alone, looking down...to see the swirling clouds parting and revealing an most amazing city. They did not have anything like this on Vantanahon. It must be from the P's travels, some of their memories leaking through. Could it be Mahavat? He'd read the histories the P's left with the first colonists here and this city looked like the images in the disked Archives. He was there; however, he was physically landing in the city. It wasn't just a re-enactment or a sharing. He was participating. He had left Vantanahon behind. He would sense that Ayah was with him and that excited him, until he felt his presence was like that of his late grandfather, in spirit only, not a physical presence.

While Rander was caught up in his travel reverie, Edelphia stood tense, palms wet, back and breasts sweaty. Eyes squeezed tight, she wondered if she'd even register an inspiration in this hopped up state. She no longer doubted her role on this mission, thanks to Sen, and she had developed an appreciation for Ashtu she had not had before. She could see Durmah warming to little Ashtu as well and that made her feel good, until she felt the sun on her face and no more inspiration than those comforting realizations.

It was Lucrea who was to have the clearest and most intense message from Jesicaahn today. She had been prepared for more insight into her role as mediator between Ashtu and Durmah and assistant to Sen and now moral and emotional support for her brother, with Ayah's time coming. She was not prepared for the Osmandeshvahan-the call to vocation that was received only by a small percentage of the population. It came in a morning's inspiration and it laid out to the recipient what Jesicaahn had in mind for that person's life's work.

Joining the Osmands meant devoting one's life to the cause, like the monks and nuns of old Mahavat, not allowing distraction in relationship or career. The community took care of the Osmands while they carried out their duties. Lucrea saw that she would need to devote her healing powers to the maintenance of the fix, once they figured out just how to fix the energy leakage. It would require most of her time and energy spent in meditation.

Initially, it seemed like a lot to ask. She'd always thought so, whenever she saw an Osmand going about his or her work. To devote one's entire life to one thing, sacrificing personal pleasure and motivation. Imagine.

Durmah wondered if he'd see more flowers as he closed his eyes in preparation for this morning's rising. Their memory was still fresh in his mind and the act of merely closing his eyes would bring them back. He'd been doing it throughout the day, even to the neglect of his duties. He'd been glad Ede hadn't asked him to go along and look for Sen. He knew this was a new experience and he'd let himself indulge a day, but it would have to stop. He would not let flowers interfere with his reason for being here on this mission.

He closed his eyes to the rising light and they appeared, brilliant and varied, but as he saw their beauty, he saw them fade and turn brown and black. Some grew green bulbous heads which themselves turned brown and black. He was horrified. Was this an omen? Some of the brown heads began to open and out came seeds, some on wings, some on little parachutes, some round, some star-shaped...flying and popping, going everywhere. What had been a field of color had turned into a field of ruin and now a sea of flying debris. It was then that he realized the fleeting beauty of the flower, how it fades and dies out and how it is reborn through the seeds it releases upon its death. So alien a concept here on Vantanahon where everything remained green and fresh and renewed itself discreetly, not in such an extravagant dance of beauty, death and rebirth. Could the very order of things be changing?

Sen was holding Ashtu as they continued to face Schmanaha rising over the nearing Kayonah Mountains. It seemed fitting that they'd be heading in that direction. It was a different world he had seen than the one he knew with his friends. He knew life was all about change, its Jesicaahn's unstoppable and inevitable nature, and yet so much change at once was overwhelming.

After everyone told of his or her inspiration they all wondered about a world without Ayah, with Rander gone, somewhere he was not sure where, Lucrea an Osmand, Durmah an animal advocate and Ede...Sen and a Ka Daklu with Ede? And a baby? Not his or hers, but Rander's? Them both raising the little boy while his father was off Vaya! Knows where? It was too strange. What did all this have to do with the mission? How could they possibly accept it as a future, but what did it have to do with their present, with what they had to accomplish on this mission? The others would certainly see Ede differently now and Rander, he'd need to find out if he knew where he was going and how it was related to healing the planet. Sen held Ashtu in the same way he held Rander's son in the image he'd just seen.

Shitsmayeh DO!

"We have to leave now!? Ayah suddenly barked.

Everyone's eyes widened on hearing Ayah's command and seeing the newly risen light disappear from the sky. Looking in the direction of the second sun, they saw Schmanaha disappear as quickly as it had risen behind the banks of dark clouds racing in from the direction of the Kayonah mountains. Lightening flashed and a wind came out of no where, tearing at their clothes and hair and sending leaves and branches flying through the air in all directions. Seven hearts sank in unison as they recognized the beginnings of the worst atmospheric disturbance on Vantanahon.

"Shitsmayeh!" shouted Durmah and they all instinctively ran for cover. "We need to reach the base of the mountains. It will be safest there. I estimate we have about an hour. Normally it would take three from here. Run!"

"Shitsmayeh Do!" shouted Rander as Ayah just stood there. "The storm is coming!"

and Durmah shouted, "Run!'"

The people of Vantanahan knew the Shitsmayeh well. Each region had its own variety of storm, and the ones near the Kayonah were the worst. Extreme winds, head-sized hail, thunder and lightening, and the ultimate deluge of rain made these storms one of the few killing forces on Vantanahan. They came up suddenly, usually at the rising of the second sun, the interaction of warm and cool air, the snow-capped Kayonah pulling these forces over them like a blanket to be unfurled over the plains leading up to their base. That's why the mountains themselves usually provided the best protection from the Shitsmayeh at their base. This time, however, the Shitsmayeh and the Kayonah were ahead of them. Running for the best cover would mean running right into the storm. By the time they reached the mountains, the storm would be behind them. The nearby trees would have to do.

"Ayah!" Rander was set to run after the others when he felt a calm hand on his arm.

"We won't all survive this one," he pronounced soberly. "We have to help them with the body transport. Now's as good a time as any for you to learn it. I had meant to teach it to you yesterday evening, but the excitement of the Presence distracted me. I don't think I would have time to move them all to the safety of the deep forest by myself."

Rander was thrilled and horrified at the same time. Use of the body transfer was not allowed on this mission and Ayah knew it. How could he be serious?! Rander's respect for the Rules, always in conflict with Ayah's defiance of them, overwhelmed his yearning to be able to learn what he'd been longing to be taught for such a long time.

Ayah felt his turmoil and said, realizing they may just need their help, "and I think you need to activate the P now. This is an emergency. We can use all the help we can get."

"Activate the...now?" Rander of course had been preparing for the P's eventual activation but he thought he had weeks, not minutes to prepare. "I will activate the P, but I will not allow you to use the body transfer now." He said matter-of-factly and initiated the contact opening without a moment's hesitation. "It won't be long now till..."

Ayah saw Rander's face go blank and saw the metallic flicker in his eyes as he looked into them and thought, no need to waste time with speech, 'Emergency! We must do body transport; this is the procedure.' He telepathed to the P inside of Rander.

Rander listened as if from the audience and understood the techniques as they were ingrained into this experience, " So, it's as simple as that,' he thought, ' an infant could do it.' And then, with the P's insight, he realized why using the body transfer now would be a disaster. "The P will not allow it." Rander told Ayah, a little dizzy with his power over his mentor's authority.

"Then you will be responsible for their deaths." Ayah proclaimed and started running towards the trees alone, leaving Rander to fend for himself.

Almost a Narrow Escape

Durmah took off first to signal the direction and once the trail and destination became obvious, he jogged off to the right to let the others pass and make sure they were all accounted for. Ede was first past him, followed closely by Sen and Lucrea neck and neck, Ashtu clinging to Sen's pack making eerie eye-contact with Durmah as they streaked by. He looked for Ayah and Rander, but they were not to be seen. He was just about to go after them when the first hail stones fell, missing him by a hair. He looked after the others and saw Ede go down as a hail stone came crashing down on her head. Then he saw Ayah running towards her and Rander just standing there. He took off after Sen and Lucrea to try to ward off any more damage.

"Head for cover of the nearest tree!" He shouted. "Keep your heads protected. Ede's already down. Ayah is with her. They dove off either side of the trail into the adjacent forest just as the trees swayed and began breaking in the rising gale and the torrents of rain replaced the huge hail balls now littering the ground in orderly rows and abstract patterns, some whole, others smashed to chunks. They were washed into piles and soon were melted by the rain. Durmah watched breathless as Lucrea dove under fallen log angled onto a boulder, followed closely by Sen and Ashtu and then, frozen as he saw a huge pine falling over on him, he disappeared with the sound of a huge crash and thud.

Durmah reappeared in the deep forest, safely removed from the tempest wailing all around them outside. Ede was supine on a sleeping pad with Ayah attending her. "We won't have much time," urged Ayah. The hail hit her straight on the top of her skull, so the damage to the brain is severe. I've reshaped her skull and was able to mentally repair the tissue, but only a bonding with a Sensitive will make it stick. I obviously am not a candidate with my short-livedness. "That leaves Sen…"

"How can this be?" frowned Durmah. "Transport is forbidden during the mission and you have transported two of us here…"

"Really Durmah, we don't have time to debate what has been done. Sen needs to be brought here as quickly as possible. Can you tell me where he is?"

"I saw Lucrea and then Sen dive under a tree on the outskirts of the forest, just before…"

"I was too busy transporting you out from under that tree, sensing your immediate danger." Ayah recalled, looking into Durmah's worried eyes.

"To the left of the place you took me," Durmah informed him reluctantly. He began to see how Ayah was creating his own fate by challenging the Fates and breaking the rules.

Sen, Lucrea and Ashtu all appeared in a flash and Ayah explained what needed to happen as quickly as he could through telepathy to Sen. "Are you willing to do this, Sen?"

"I just saw it this morning in my inspiration, the Ka Daklu with Ede – how can I refuse?" Sen looked at Lucrea and she too saw what needed to be done. She knelt on Ede's right. "I just wish it could be done under less fatal circumstances."

"I can perform the ceremony," Ayah was already preparing himself. Lucrea can be the Side since she's experienced it at our Ka Daklu. Ayah stood and closed his eyes and out of his mouth, came a sound like "Ohm." It's reverberation off the nearby old growth put everyone into a sort of trance. Taking his cue, Sen put one hand on Ede's head and with the other held her left hand. He too closed his eyes and opened his mouth, his vocalization blending in with Ayah's, which had not stopped. Lucrea took the right hand and followed their example. Soon three voices were harmonizing in Ohms. Ayah then stopped, leaving the other two voices duet and knelt, putting one of his hands on each of their hearts.

He then initiated the specific Ka Daklu chant mentally and then added its words to the Ohm-chant of the other two. Durmah was kneeing nearby with his eyes closed when he felt a vibration starting in the base of his spine and moving up to the top of his head. They all experienced the shiver of the force, and with a deep intake of oxygen, it was completed." Sen and Ede were now as one.

The Consequences of Their Actions

"What just happened?" Durmah asked Lucrea, reeling from the vibrations still.

"You have just witnessed the Ka Daklu, the ritual joining of Sen and Ede." Lucrea mouthed the words as if trying them out. Were they really true?

"The Ka Daklu binds two souls together. Usually it's used for couples wanting to cement their relationship spiritually as well as socially. It has also life saving powers. When bonded to a sensitive, a person in mortal danger can be healed by the vibrations of the chant." Ayah's mind wandered as he tried to explain to Durmah what he had just experienced.

Neither Durmah nor Lucrea were happy with this sudden turn of events. Durmah had been sleeping with Ede, just the night before, now she and Sen were bonded together. Lucrea knew Sen was Sumitrahn, but she'd grown fond of him and Ashtu and held on to her own hopes. These furtive hopes were now dashed, like Ede's head, which was the cause of this whole mess. And what of Ashtu? The Ka Daklu demanded total and exclusive bonding of the two participants for the first two years. No other close personal relationships were allowed, human or animal. They were deemed too distracting and that period of time was needed to meld the two souls into a perfect harmony.

Durmah had never seen a Ka Daklu before, though he had imagined doing one someday, maybe even with Ede. So much for that plan. Lucrea's only consolation was that she assumed she'd be Ashtu's next human companion.

Ede was next in line to be shocked. She slowly opened her eyes to see Sen at her side and Lucrea and Ayah nearby. Sen was holding her hand and his other hand sat warmly on her aching head. "What just happened? One moment I was running and getting pounded by gigantic hail and the next I'm under this huge tree with Sen holding my hand and..." she stopped, eyes wide with understanding. "And the next I've done the Ka Daklu with Sen?! How is this possible?"

"Let me explain," started Lucrea quietly and Sen looked at these two closely.

"What's the penalty for breaking the rules of the mission?" Durmah asked, though he already knew the answer and looked at Ayah, giving up his hope of saving him from the death he'd already seen.

Rander and the P

The P now activated, Rander saw his future laid out, including his improbable and seemingly impossible impregnation of Ede to produce their next carrier. He and the P within him realized what Ayah had done. The penalty for breaking such rules is extreme. He crouched in the forest's periphery waiting for the Shitsmayeh to pass and moved his thoughts out to locate the others. He sensed them under a huge tree in the forest's core and felt the Ka Daklu being done between Ede and Sen. He saw too how Ayah's stubborn, yet brave action to save members of the mission had sealed his fate, a self-fulfilling prophesy of sorts. 'It's a form of suicide,' he wondered out loud.

The P directed him to their exact location after the hail ended, though the pouring rain. Rander and the P came up slowly and knelt by Ede's side. He started to explain to her what his inspiration that morning had been.

She saw it too as she looked into his eyes, dancing with silver flecks. She closed hers and slept some to escape and digest her new course in life. The others saw the change in Rander, too. It was not only the strangely alluring metallic, mechanical flicker in his eyes, it was also something about his overall demeanor, his gait, his carriage. Like his eyes, it was strangely appealing, disconcertingly alien.

"Where is my Rander?" asked Ayah as he observed the changes while Rander squatted near Ede, asleep in her state of being overwhelmed.

"I'm still here." Silver flecks in his eyes dancing in discernable patterns. "I just have company, now and there's room for us all. Don't worry, no one gets lost in the activation." His voice echoed now with the reverberations of thousands of memories. "Ayah, what you have done...?"

"Yes. I must answer to the Budhaun and to the P," mouthed Ayah, still defiant. "I could not, would not not do what I knew I must not do."

For Rander, with the P activated, it was like being in a room full of people. In his head, projected both inwards and outwards were hundreds of stimulating conversations, videos and music playing all around, an academic lecture and a trip through the stars, all going on at the same time. It was like being at a huge, fantastic party only he had access to each and every conversation and event. It took some getting used to. Yes, he felt different and no, he would never want it any other way, ever. It was like tripping out on some particularly good mushroom from the forest he was flying around. In fact, he could see just the ones, here and there, spot-lit and magnificent.

The aftermath of the recent storm had entered the center of the woods by then with rain and a slowed-down wind, but the huddled masses felt safe and cozy under the shelter of their treed refuge in which they'd been transported to and gathered together at by Ayah.

"I think I know the answer to this question," began Durmah "But why couldn't you have just transported us all the way to Indrasiah, while you were at it? We could be working on the fix rather than being holed up here, helpless and useless, waiting out a Shitsmayeh."

"Shitsmayeh Do! Shitsmayeh Do!" sang out Rander, dancing around the biggest tree, twirling and then levitating like a Shitsmayeh of his own creation.

The others looked at him and at each other wide-eyed.

"Looks like the P are waking up and enjoying the extremes of our dilemma." Sen was watching the glowing sparks in Rander's eyes as they swung by him in their revolutions.

"Back to Durmah's question, part of getting to the end is the means. The way we get to Indrasiah, what we're experiencing now, as a group and all that we are experiencing individually, Ede, Sen and Rander spinning with the Parushaha aware and excited to be freed in human form, are part of the eventual solution – fuel for the fire. Things we would not go through if we all transported in seconds to our destination. That's why Ayah's impetuous decision to use the body transport, even though well-intentioned, carries with it such serious consequences. He was charged by the Budhaun as the leader of this mission and such a miscalculation could not only endanger the mission, but carries with it the death sentence, rarely used on Vantanahan." Ayah was standing with his back to the group, silently fuming, as Sen gave his run-down of the current mess he'd gotten them all into.

'I feel so alone,' thought Ayah, 'with Rander taken over by the P and my decision putting the mission at risk…' He had begun to doubt the nobleness of his decision to risk his life to save Ede's and maybe some of the others, like Durmah, as well. On the other hand, as was predicted in Sen's morning inspiration, Jesicaahn had this all planned out for reasons of her own. Somehow, his death figured into the big picture. Had he screwed it up? So far, it all seemed to be jiving well with each person's inspiration. In addition, he really didn't believe that any individual's action could possibly go against the Will of Jesicaahn. That is just arrogance and ego talking.

Ashtu, Rander and the P

Ashtu leapt onto Rander's back and hung on with claws extended, enjoying the ride and accepting the presence of the P unconditionally and with glee. Lucrea and Sen watched intently and tried to ascertain the connections, the significance of what they were witnessing. Why would there be an attraction of a meerkat to a mechanical presence like the P? Why were the P enjoying corporal form, almost in a possession-like way, so much? Was it in that DNA incorporated into the P's makeup by Yeshmani? Could there be some reconnection at the genetic level accentuated by a lifetime in dormancy? And most importantly, how could they use this to fix an energy leak on the planetary level?

Durmah, on a simple level, was also interested in the impromptu dance show. How was it that Ashtu had access to information, intuition, which he did not? That little creature was just full of surprises. He was now just beginning to see its value.

Ede opened her eyes and closed them again at the sight of Rander and Ashtu flying around the tree canopy. She'd heard about levitation, but had never seen it before. This was getting stranger and stranger by the minute and she was not yet ready to take part in the craziness.

As suddenly as it came upon them on the trail, Shitsmayeh Na, the end of the storm, descended – the skies cleared and the wind died down to its usual steady blow. There was never a lot of stillness on Vantanahon, which was why their time in the deep forest under the tree, hours of it, ultimately made them all anxious to get going again. Stillness in the middle of the waking daylight hours was one of the most alien of feelings for these people and aside from the P through Rander, everyone was anxious to be out in the steady breeze again. Rander had collapsed from exhaustion after the P had had their fill of this new experience, allowing this new body to rest, digesting its limits as well as benefits.

The suns came out, bathing the mountains in light and the group emerged from the forest into this light to calculate how far they had come and where to go next. Ayah and Durmah walked up the trail to look at the canyon walls ahead leading deep into the Kayonah. Ede and Lucrea looked back and saw the spot where the hail hit and Ayah stepped in, bringing them here.

"It will still take us most of the day to get up there." She evaluated. "In a way, Shitsmayeh did us a favor, we'll have more energy for the mountains after the enforced rest period." Lucrea for her part was glad to see her awake and coping again with things at hand.

The group headed up the trail which led up the canyon into the Kayonah. Here they could run into the Adrija, the mountain-born, those who chose to live more secluded lives sequestered in the valleys and canyons of the Kayonah.

Durmah had heard of the Adrija, but had never seen one of them. He was playing with the idea that the Presence the other night may have been one of them when they heard a shout from high above them.

"Welcome travelers. We saw you coming and then escaping the Shitsmayeh. You must have great power traveling with you. We are honored and I can be your Metra (guide) in the Kayonah. They can be confusing to navigate at times. In a second she was gone, only to reappear through a heretofore unnoticeable gap in the stone wall to the right of the path. Before Durmah could open his mouth, the woman had laid her hand on his arm, a symbol of respect and peace and said, "Don't worry, I know you are their Metra, I don't desire to usurp your position, just augment it. My name is Rosediah Shanti. Welcome."

Rosediah Shanti

She stood there, a head taller than anyone in the group, including Rander, who was taller than most Vantanahans. Her hair was a kaleidoscope of colors, accentuating her dark skin and perfect complexion. She looked ageless, adult and strong, but anywhere from 20-40, depending on the light. Her body was strong and well-formed and her legs were displayed, distending from short pants, unheard of in other parts of the planet. She had a bow across her back and a buff-colored, leather-fringed top. Rosediah was a knock-out.

"They grow 'em big here in the mountains," observed Ede, not noticeably the shortest one present.

"They grow them big where you're from," quipped Rosediah, eyeing her breasts.

"They also grow 'em Hanahan, in case you're interested." Durmah's eyebrow raised comically at hearing Ede's comment. He was already 'rising to the occasion' of working with a fellow guide, especially such a substantially impressive one.

"I'll keep that in mind," snickered Ede, "For the time being, I'm occupied, and she glanced at Sen and looked for Rander, acknowledging for the first time, their new and future connections.

Rosediah took all this in and thought, 'An emergency Ka Daklu has just been performed here. Interesting...and an ill-advised use of the transport by Ayah. I can see I'll have my work cut out for me with this group.'

'Indeed you will,' returned Sen in thought alone and she glanced at him in mild surprise.

"Sensitives, too! Well this is a welcome surprise. You must show me Ayah! I was the one who did the Ka Daklu for him and...'

"Rander at your service," he said bowing and she looked into his eyes with surprise and recognition.

"So there you are, Rander! Ayah! So nice to see you again." She hugged them both together in a great embrace. "I have a dozen or so questions, not the least of which is your decision to use the transport, even in a Shitsmayeh. They can wait. Let me lead you all to the next pass where we have a shelter and can enjoy some Adrijan hospitality." The fact that Rosediah knew of the serious condition affecting Ayah, yet still put hospitality first, was early proof of this custom.

They walked on steadily for the rest of the day and as the first sun set, they could see strange lights up ahead.

"Luminaries," Rosediah began to explain and Rander added "The technology of the P...I see whole cities glowing at night in light. I can even see how it's done. Why is it that we don't have that technology in Ojaswan?"

For the first time, Rander spoke the name of the place they all came from, the grasslands settlement of Ojaswan. They had no fires nor artificial lighting to keep away the darkness. When the suns set, it was the end of their day and their work. It was also why they rose so early and made such a ceremony of the two suns rising. Was it also why they had the inspiration? Ojaswan in old Sanskrit am means 'vital energy.'

Their forefathers believed in living in tune with nature and following all of nature's rules, so no meat-eating, no technology to enhance their lives, only the vital energies of Jesicaahn, Schmanaha and Deshmaha. Being the keepers of the Archives, they know in detail how the abuse of the planet had let to their home world's destruction. We did their best not to let that happen to Vantanahon. Their power came not from the planet but from the healers in the Rhetiorma, and the power of Swastia and the Osmandeshvahan, and the rules of the Budhaun all designed to sustain them and purify them in their austere dedication. Now, they were being exposed to the world outside their rigid aesthecism. Maybe that's why Rosediah seemed less preoccupied with the consequences of using the transport than with offering them Adrijan hospitality.

Rosediah led them into the strangely lit room as the darkness made them all want to call it quits for the day. What they saw inside, however, woke them up like cold water in the face. Suddenly, they were energized and not sleepy in the least.

The ceiling of the one-room structure was high and steeped. From the center hung the light source, or four of them, suspended on a cross-shape about five heads above Rosediah who strode to the center and beckoned the others to follow – join her. Every corner seemed lit and on the far wall, a roaring fire added its own ambiance to the scene. For the second time, the traditional Ojaswans were taken aback, then pleased by the burning of wood. On low banquettes around the walls, other Adrija lay sprawled on the couches and got up, one by one, as the group entered. They were all as tall and as strikingly beautiful as Rosediah. Each one greeted each new comer warmly, first taking their hands, clasped in between their two hands and held long, while looking deeply into each others eyes. After they got a feel for who the person was that they were meeting, they would hug the new acquaintance strongly and each new traveler would feel an overwhelming sense of connection and peace and welcome to this new community.

After formal introductions, each Adrijan led one of their guests to a banquette and let them know that that would be their resting place for the evening and that each would have an Adrijan sleeping partner as part of the hospitality service. Though a pleasing prospect to most, it became a dilemma for Sen and Ede who'd just been bonded that day with the Ka Daklu. Sleeping together was part of the ceremony, especially on the first night and here they were with the unusual hospitality of the Adrija and conflicting sleeping options. Ayah saw it immediately and pulled Rosediah aside to tell her.

"I can see we have some cultural differences," she began pleasantly. "I expected them to appear when I first heard of your coming through the Kayonah. I didn't expect them to arise so quickly, however, and I was not prepared to a Ka Daklu couple and an animal companion.

"I'm sorry, there was not time to give you an update since we left," Ayah had contacted Rosediah out of protocol to let her know they'd be passing through her region. At that time, there was no Ka Daklu outside of his and Rander's, which Rosediah had presided at and therefore knew about and no meerkat additions. He had already sensed the anxious response to Ashtu's presence in the hut.

The solution was simple enough. The new Ka Daklu was explained to all and the need for privacy understood by the Adrija and since Ashtu was used to sleeping in trees, it only followed that the three would sleep outside, the newly Ka-Daklued in their compartment and Ashtu perched in the trees above, thereby diffusing any issues with either. It was agreed that someone should be on the look-out for the return of the Presence anyway. Everyone seemed pleased with the outcome. Ayah snuggled down with Rosediah, Durmah with her sister, and Rander with her brother and Lucrea with a cousin. Talk went on late until Rosediah gave the signal for lights out. Like a sudden sunset, it became dark and still, quiet as the deep forest in full suns.

It had been awhile since Ayah had slept with a woman, but the Adrija were so adept at the skill of hospitality that he barely missed Rander's feel and smell so near. He and his partner had agreed that for the sake of protocol, they could forego their Ka Daklu sleep requirements for one night, even though their nights were numbered. Rosediah's choice of sleeping partner for Rander made the latter acquiesce much more readily that he normally would.

Durmah was unclear if sex would be a part of this sleeping arrangement, but he doubted it considering there was no privacy at all in this one room cabin. Lucrea felt less left out being pared up as she was and Rander was enjoying the feel of another man in his arms. It had been awhile and he forgot how he loved the newness and discovery of a new body's terrain.

Outside was another story. Sen and Ede finally had to deal with the reality of their new situation. Frankly, they were both relieved to be so exhausted from the day. It made things less intimate to be so tired, their exhaustion lending an air of normalcy to a day which had not been normal in the slightest. They both lay on their backs, looking up at the nearness of the curved roof of their sleeping compartment. Sen would be the first to break the silence.

"Any ideas as to how to play this?" he asked hopefully, since he was all out of ideas.

"We just go one night at a time." Ede snuggled up to Sen's warmth, which relaxed them both. "I understand the logic of having to go this route, and it did save my life after all. Thanks by the way; I don't know if I properly thanked you for your part in this. It's quite a sacrifice you made to help my existence to continue. As for how we play this, we can improvise, hybridize, and come up with some combo that works for us in our situation without officially violating the rules." The lasses faire attitude of the Adrija was attractive and Ede saw the sense in being flexible. "I know I owe you my life and for the time being, need you to sustain it."

"And the baby by Rander?"

"One life-altering change at a time, Sen. These are just images and so far, I have not been privy to any of them. Who knows what will actually happen. We'll deal with that one when and if it comes. Right now, I'm just happy to be out from under those strange lights and in the cozy dark with two souls I know and can relate to."

"That is something I can relate to as well." Sen breathed as he snuggled with one female, knowing the other was stationed in the tree above, watchful in the peaceful dark of the Kayonah.

Everything seems better in the morning. You're not all tired from the day you've previously survived and you have new energy to deal with what life has to throw at you in the new day. These thoughts were going through the travelers' minds as they all got up quietly and gathered outside for the sunrise. Being in the mountains, it was later than on the plains. They sensed it being up but could not yet see the actual rising of the first sun. It was off-putting. They all felt a little late. By the time the sun did peak over the peaks, they were noticeably anxious.

"Look at them standing out there fidgeting," said Rosediah's brother as they stood together at the shelter's front winder. Everyone was still asleep. "Rander is such a presence that no matter how quiet he'd be, I would feel his departure. What are they doing?"

"It's a ritual they have. They greet the suns every morning and get their inspiration for the day. It's especially important when they're on a mission like this one."

"Why don't we do it? Is it a thing just for the Ojaswan people?"

"I'm not sure. They are much more in tune with nature than even we are, with no fire and no artificial lighting allowed. Humans also develop habits and traditions based on their environment. The suns make up more of the plains peoples' day. I think they are so agitated now because the sun's rise is later here in the Kayonah. I wonder how that will affect their inspirations.

"I think I want to go with them." Rosediah looked at her brother with surprise on her brows.

A Kayonah Inspiration on Day 3

Sandaram the beautiful, the handsome. That was Rosediah's brother's name and he was who Rander saw shining in his inspiration. There was no Ayah, no Ka Daklu. Only Sandaram, he and Rander on a Khaga, a trip through the stars.

Ayah saw them all moving away from him-it seemed that he no longer needed any inspiration, so, eyes opened, he watched the others receive theirs. He saw surprise and pleasure on Rander's face and sensed he'd be well taken care of and was now finding out by whom. Sen and Ede's expressions were identical, not surprising, since they now shared a fate. Lucrea looked perplexed and he knew her road would not be easy. She would be separated from those she loved. Durmah looked at peace and full of confidence and pride. Ayah wished that Durmah could be the one there for Lucrea, but he saw Durmah's path down a separate road.

As Deshmaha rose on this, the third day of their journey to Indrasiah, everyone opened their eyes and looked around and then at Ayah, standing alone with tears coming down from his hooded eyes. Rander went to hug him and the others, even Durmah joined in.

"Thank you for that. I feel so alone moving on to another plane, but it looks as if we are all moving on in directions we had not anticipated.

Sandaram

It was to everyone's (except maybe Rander's) surprise that Sandaram had requested and gotten Ayah's permission to join the mission. "It only makes sense that all the planetary citizens who can, take part in an attempt to put this right, in this out-of-balance situation."

Rosediah had approached Ayah after they returned from the Inspiration and he was only a bit surprised by the request. He was pained by the developing attraction between Rander and Sandaram, but both he and Rander did need to move on and Ka Daklu or not, it was good for Rander of find someone new; he was not one to be alone. Where Ayah was going, being alone was the name of the game. With a twinge of jealousy and what-about-my-needs, fleeting though they may be, Ayah acquiesced. It did make sense, as Rosediah presented it, and they could use all the help and diversity of talent that they could get. Who knew how many more Vantanahans they'd pick up by the time they reached Indrasiah?

So, now they were eight, counting Ashtu. Sandaram had his own Adrijan sleeping compartment and Ayah marveled at the jostling of pairings from just three days of travel. From the original teams of Rander/Ayah, Durmah/Ede, Lucrea/Senthion/Ashtu, it would soon evolve into Rander/Sandaram, Senthion/Ede, Durmah/Ashtu and Ayah/Lucrea. Ayah knew of Lucrea's possible future as an Osmand, so this style of traveling would be their last, and they made the most of it whenever they could.

On an average, daily stroll through life, most people you see are just average looking. Some better looking, others less attractive, but every once in awhile, nature rolls double sixes, or snake-eyes if you prefer, and a real beauty is born. Nature has always done this – the odds are that a true beauty will emerge each generation.

Though Rander was tall, blond and handsome, he dimmed in Sandaram's light. It was obvious from the beginning, thus the name he was given. His father was quite handsome and his mother a beauty, but nothing in comparison to what their son would be. They, and everyone else, marveled that they had produced such a creature. Each year, he seemed to grow more and more striking. His hair, like his sisters, had every color from blond to black, it changed in the light and with the season. His eyes were similarly colored, blue, green, brown, violet, black, flecks of sliver dancing, since he was a carrier of the P as well. He'd had to activate them early on to save his people from an avalanche that buried them all one winter when he was only three. He became even more beautiful in the eyes of his people after that. He grew tall, broad in shoulder, narrow in waist, walking gracefully on strong perfectly formed legs. His hands made people either weep or cum.

With beauty can come loneliness. Sanda had never had a lover because no one had dared approach him. He had met his match in Rander, who had never not had a lover because with his particular brand of beauty, came an innate ability to please and put people at ease. Sanda had not had a chance, but to fall under his spell. Rander for the first time in his life was not in control and this loss of himself to another was such a turn-on that he all but forgot about the Ka Daklu. He saw it pained Ayah and at the same time, knew that Ayah had already moved on emotionally to that higher plain that he would soon leave his physical body behind to ascent to. In this changed state of affairs, in steps Sanda, corporal, attractive and aching to be loved by another man in a way he had not yet experienced. Rander was beside himself. Lucrea was beside herself as well, forsaking her traditional spot by his side.

Sandaram was the perfect guide through the Kayonah and he and Durmah had a lot in common. Though he was Mahantahn, Durmah could see the attraction Sandaram commanded. It was not lost on Lucrea, either; who was the perpetual odd-man-out was getting annoyed with her brother, who now seemed to have two bed mates.

"Rander, this is unseemly, you fawning over this guy while Ayah looks on sadly, stoically, with resignation."

"Have you seen Sanda, really? Looked into his eyes, Lucrea?"

"Are you so shallow, brother, as to be so turned by just a pretty face?" Lucrea could be the latent Osmand in her judging and feeling the need to lecture. "Vaya Rander, Ayah is not dead yet, and what about the Ka Daklu? What is it with you and Sandaram?"

"You've never taken an interest in my sex life before, little sister, why now?" Rander himself was wondering about his actions. Even he was not this hedonistic. Could it have to do with both of them having activated P's? Were the P's attracted to each other?

"It's just not fair!" blurted out a green-with-envy Lucrea. "There I said it. I'm jealous of you and your two lovers; with me all alone and destined for Osmandhood. Can't I have a little attention shown me in my last days of freedom?"

"We haven't yet talked about you as an Osmand. It seems so extreme...I think we both need a breath of fresh air and a better world view."

Rander swept Lucrea off her feet and in seconds the two were on top of the Kayonah's highest peak, looking out over the sea. "This is what is important now." He said pointing across the sea to the mists of Indrasiah. "Thank you for pointing out my distraction and getting my mind back on my role in this mission."

"When did you learn how to do this?" began Lucrea, referring to the transport.

"I've been after Ayah to teach me for moons now. Then yesterday, when the Shitsmayeh hit, it said it was time. I disagreed, knowing the consequences of breaking the no-transport rule. After wanting something for so long, there I was in the situation of feeling the need to turn it down...the time wasn't right."

"So what happened? Ayah did use it to transport Ede and then Sen and I," was Lucrea's next question.

"I did agree it was time to activate the P, and I was overwhelmed by them just as Ayah conveyed the instructions. They agreed that it should not be used. I learned the method, and it's really so simple, but stayed behind, did not use it. This is the first time I have actually put it to use. This ability, not to mention the presence of the P, is changing me..."

"Does it make you feel more powerful?"

"Power is an issue right now, but more so with the P. I feel so elevated by their knowledge and presence. There are things they can learn from me, too--like this transport. There is too much going on right now. I'm at the verge of being overwhelmed, knowing I'll lose Ayah, you know how much the Ka Daklu meant to me and now, I see how basically flawed my thinking was. There is no contract, written or verbal that can validate, solidify, or perpetuate people's feelings. They change, evolve and won't be made static by anything, not even a Ka Daklu. Maybe that's my lesson in all this. Then, there's Sanda. His beauty and strength feed me; they are so new and refreshing- like this mountain air. How can I turn away from that? I know the timing is off-even wrong, but there are no accidents. I believe that."

"We do have choices, though," Lucrea stood next to Rander, listening to him move away from her, spiritually, emotionally and soon physically. He took her hand and they stood in silence. She was actually thinking more about her situation and the Osmandeshvahan. It's so hard to focus on the others. Just as quickly as they came, they were back on the spot they'd left.

Just then, Sanda appeared over the top, panting. She saw the P in his eyes and realized that even for a veteran Osmand; Rander would be a lost cause.

"Rander, here is where you have gotten off to. I need to run. Come on down for a run with me! We can scout up ahead on the trail."

"He likes to run, too!" Rander giggled joyously and the two were off, leaving Lucrea to marvel at the synchronicity of the two beauties.

Sanda and Durmah led everyone down from the Kayonah to the sacred forest of the Nish Para Acala', the land of boundless nature. The trees stretched in a band as far as the eye could see from the lower slopes of the mountains to the beach a mile away-an undulating blanket of greens and grays and silvers of all shades. The trees in this area were Eucalypti, one of the species brought with the colonists from the Home Planet. The trunks were silver white and the leaves greenish silver. They emitted an enchanting smell which encouraged people to linger and soak up the healing energies being emitted. This was Ayah's home and he felt recharged just being back in his trees.

From high on the mountains, the travelers gasped at the first sight of the green belt of forest, with the startling violet colored water beyond. The make up of the atmosphere on Vantanahan colored the sky various shades and the current color also tinted the waters. They stood like trees themselves rooted in the beauty of the moment —one fleeting vision of Jesicaahn that they would never recapture, exactly, again.

"Your homeland is stunning, Ayah," gasped Rander as he hugged his departing soul mate. Ayah smoothed Rander's hair and held him close as he silently thanked Jesicaahn for the welcome and farewell gift.

Durmah asked Sanda about their night visitor. Sanda's beautiful eyes widened and Durmah was mesmerized by the dance of light and color. What did they remind him of the flowers? So caught up in the eyes and colors and flowers, Durmah missed Sanda's question to him. "I'm sorry, what was that?"

"I asked you if it felt malevolent." Sanda seemed unaware of his effect on the people around him. It wasn't as much about being oblivious as it was being genuine.

"Well it did knock Ashtu out of her tree perch."

"It could have been as simple as Saswati watching out for her forest or..."

"You mean Saswati spirits exist? I thought they were only children stories."

"We tell them to the children to develop their respect for nature-but they do exist especially in the old growth. They are who the Sensitives commune with when they go off in to the woods."

"I would assume that Sen or Ayah would have identified it at such then." Reasoned Durmah, continuing hesitantly, "You mentioned the Saswati and then you said, 'or...'"

The light dimmed a shade in Sanda's eyes and it was Durmah's eye's turn to widen, "I would rather not even put the energy out there involved in postulating the 'or' possibility. But I will keep tuned in and if threat is what is following, all will need to know and be prepared." With that comment, Sanda went off to be alone.

Senthion and Ayah rushed ahead like little boys at heart when they entered the forests of Nish Para Acala'. Every once in a while, they'd stop by a particularly large and aged tree and press their foreheads against its trunk, shivering in the energy jolt they'd get. Sanda and the others watched them in amusement and Rander tried the forehead thing and came away, shaking his head.

"Nothing?" asked Ede, her ego still smarting. "I can relate to that."

"Not everyone is as open as the Sensitives," Sanda put a hand on each one's shoulder, standing in the middle, "I can show you some opening techniques," he offered.

"Oh, I'd love that," gushed Ede and Rander's P sparks literally jumped the distance from his eyes to Sanda's and Sanda's Ps likewise jumped to Rander's eyes.

"Are your P's doing a Tandara?" asked Ede, referring to the traditional dance in which teams from two tribes line up and dance back and forth, exchanging greetings and energy with their partner's team.

"That's a good way of putting it. We notice that we have different information and points of view, from one set of P to another. It's fascinating. They are learning from each other just as we are learning from them.

The P in Rander were thrilled to be brought back out of statius and even more excited to meet the P of Sanda. After generations apart, parts of the mechanical collective were being reunited across the short space between the two men's eyes. They reveled in being in physical form, activating parts of their DNA long dormant in their mechanical forms as P navigators and colony seeders. When actually a part of a human organism, as they were in Rander and Sanda, they made much more sense of the theory they'd learned since their circuits were originally activated.

The human parts of Rander and Sanda stood back, amused by the excitement their mechanical companions evinced. It was only when they sensed the other's discomfort that they curbed some of the more visible displays of excitement and decided they would thereafter let the P explore more discretely at night or times when they could be alone, away from the rest of the party. Rander worried that they would overpower him, take control of all his senses, but Sanda with more activation experience, assured him that this was just the excitement of reunification. It would settle down and they'd be more in the background, just as Rander and Sanda's humanness was at the moment. In fact, it was getting hard for Rander to imagine life without the P, though when he thought about it more, he realized he'd never really known that...a life without the Parushaha inside.

They stayed in the forest to recharge before the crossing. They would go up to a clearing on a treeless hill and look at the Saragossa Sea, which was a light violet red this time of year. The colors changed with the seasonal atmosphere. The crossing would be grueling, especially for Ayah, the eldest of the group. They were required to swim to Indrasiah.

Indrasiah was a place of pilgrimage and tradition had it that one had to endure hardships to get there. Therefore, there were no boats or other means of conveyance over the Sea to Indrasiah and that's why transport was forbidden. Especially the transport Ayah had used to escape that Shitsmayeh, which was a serious break in protocol. Would the Nish Para Omatra of Indrasiah allow them to enter knowing this detail of their journey so far? Would the Budhaun carry out the rarely meted death sentence on one of their own? Durmah and Rander were worried about this as they stood looking at the length of the Sea they'd need to swim across.

"What if we make it all the way, only to be denied entry?"

"It's a chance we'll have to take," counseled Durmah, a comforting hand on Rander's arm. "There's no way for us to know that before we get there."

"Actually there is a way," began Rander "and it involved the P."

"Ah, the P," sighed Durmah, sensing more infractions coming against his sacred version of Vantanahan tradition.

As Rander thought of the body transport, which the P had discouraged him from doing since they realized the laws forbidding it, he felt the urge to explore it more. In reality, the P wanted to learn more about it. The idea of their being refused entry to Indrasiah because of Ayah's use of it occurred to them. The P asked simply, "Why don't you just ask them?"

"We won't find out till we get there, having risked our lives in the crossing."

"Why not ask them now, before you leave?"

"How?"

"Send them a message."

The P were used to electronic communication so sending messages was routine for them. They were also aware the low-tech level which was almost a religion on Vantanahon, to keep life natural, unaided by artificial means. There was the idea of a messenger, though. Birds have been messengers in the past, and even some sea mammals.

The P asked Rander, "Could Ayah or Senthion communicate with the species of dolphin in the Saragossa? Then, there was that presence that had spooked them back on the first night. Could it be relied upon to aid them rather than just observing and following?"

This was the first Rander heard that the presence was still following them. There had been no more sightings or feelings about it since that first night, so Rander had put it in the back of his mind. The P seemed to take it for granted that this presence was still around.

Rander approached Ayah and Sen, "We have a job for you." And he explained the P's idea about communication with the dolphins.

Meanwhile Sanda went off in search of the presence. He took Ashtu with him since she was the one with the closest contact with the whatever-it-was so far.

With Rander, Sen and Ayah off in search of the Saragossan dolphins and Sanda and Ashtu and Durmah, who decided to go along for support or protection, off in a more dangerous venture, Edie and Lucrea found themselves the lone females in the camp.

"Let's cook up a big celebration meal for when the men folk return." Ede was no cook and merely referring to some old traditions.

"Why not?" answered Lucrea, surprising Ede out of her reverie. "It'll give us a chance to get to know each other a little better. I need to ask your thoughts on my inspiration."

After hearing what Lucrea had to say, Ede said simply, "Osmandeshvahan. You really want to be an Osmand?"

"Never in my life, but it was in the Inspiration, so I imagined it's my destiny."

"Listen, Lucrea. If I looked to inspiration to determine my destiny, I'd be sitting on my ass doing nothing. I get nothing and I've accepted that, so maybe you could accept that the inspiration is just an idea. Sometimes we get ideas and some times we don't have a clue, but we live our lives anyway. We do the best we can with what we get."

"So that's your advice? Consider it a suggestion and do what I want with my life?"

"Exactly. Be free. Why be a slave to the Osmandeshvahan?"

At the beach, Sen and Ayah watched as Rander stripped down to his beautiful nakedness and walked confidently into the warm sea waters. They looked at each other with admiration and a bit of jealousy in their eyes and shed their clothes to follow him. All Vantanahans are excellent swimmers, having learned from birth, which takes place in a special hot spring at their vortex of birth. The truly blessed, like Rander and Sanda were birthed at Indrasiah. Sen was birthed at the Vortex of Naha and Ayah was birthed at the Nish Para Acala' springs, named the Rapha. Entry into water always brings a flashback of birth to them.. They soon caught up to Rander and began to swim in a pod-like formation, one way to call the dolphins. Ayah also new some of their language and began producing the sounds that would notify the dolphin scouts of their presence and desire for contact.

Not every planet had seas and not every planet with seas had dolphins. Wherever suitable, they were considered part of the planets colonization, as they could fit in without harming or being harmed by the native life already present. The Saragossa Sea was an ideal home for them and the Saragossan pod was large and thriving. Because of their own Sensitives, whom Ayah was now contacting, they were sure they'd want to be of help to the mission.

The communication was intercepted by the Bala pod while they were doing their favorite activity, playing. In translation, here is their conversation:

"Uravahn" Ayah spoke in Balan, 'with greetings and requests'.

"Always with requests, never only greetings and play." Was the usual reply.

"Friendly, fellow inhabitants of this world."

"Prefer play."

"Always, make request into play."

"Yes, this way." They swam off jumping over each other, breaching the surface to catch a glimpse of the Uravahn pod.

After the necessary greetings and some spontaneous play, which Sen suggested and was well received by the three Balans, Ayah explained the request simply.

"Make request into play," one Balan repeated.

Rander caught on first and told Ayah his idea on how this proposition could be made into a game. "Give them each the message and a method of delivery, the winner receives a ration of their favorite fish. One will deliver a written message, another in spoken form and the third by telecommunication with the Omatra at Indrasiah. They'd have to swim together to the shores to be in communication range. They have one hour."

Back on the trail, Ashtu had taken to the trees and was on the lookout for the presence that had knocked her out of the trees that night. Sanda had followed her, at a respectful distance and Durmah marveled at their dance-like display of agility high above the forest floor. Local birds took flight, disturbedly and Durmah worried that the-whatever-it-was would not show itself in all the commotion. Still, he stood watch below, senses alert and attack-mode initiated. From up above, Ashtu chirped once and met eyes with Sanda, directing him to a spot in Durmah's blind eye. Sanda saw a motion and before he could call out, Durmah disappeared. Eyes widened, the two climbed down quickly to search the area.

"Durmah?" called Sanda tentatively, knowing his call went unheard. Ashtu sniffed the ground where they'd 'seen' the disturbance and verified to Sanda it was what she had encountered the other night. They hurried back to tell the others.

"It is as I'd feared, one of the Aja, or unborn. They are spirits of dead or unborn life forms that follow those living looking for a chance to be reborn or initially born. Usually they stay to themselves, in uninhabited regions, but once in a while, a rogue Aja will wander off.

One minute he was standing there in the forest, the next he felt a chill and realized the presence was nearby, behind him and the third minute he was gone. Now he was nowhere, all was black and he hung as if suspended, but could feel no ropes or hooks on his body, which was nude he realized nonchalantly. What had happened to his clothes? On closer inspection, he was missing more than his clothes. He didn't have his body, either. That's why he felt nude; it was basically just his consciousness here in the dark void. 'Am I dead?' he wondered. 'Is this what if feels like to be dead? Did that thing kill me? What about the others? It was my job to protect them and here I am, the first to succumb to it, without even a fight. I didn't lift as much as a finger in my defense...'

Meanwhile, Durmah's body, clothed and looking relaxed, walked into the camp just as Sanda was telling the others of his disappearance. Sanda's back was to him and the presence inside him curved up his lips into a smirk as he came up silently and stood there, watching the shock register in everyone else's eyes.

Sanda, seeing their expressions, turned around and looked into what had recently been Durmah's eyes.

"What have you done with Durmah?" he asked and everyone gasped.

The Anila (The Anila)

It/he stood facing the humans, for the first time in human form. The animal hissed at him as he remembered the other night when it'd been scared out of the tree. A smile appeared on Durmah's face and the animal seemed to calm down. It was somehow different being with them in their form. He felt less left out, less envious. It/he understood the delicate situation, however, and knew it needed to make its intentions known clearly and soon.

In Durmah's voice, accentuated by an unfamiliarity with using the equipment, he began. "The one you call Durmah, the spirit who normally dwells in this body, is secure. His spirit is...being kept safe until I have completed my mission, as you call it."

"And what is your mission?" asked Lucrea, uncharacteristically aggressive. Ede raised an eyebrow, having never heard that tone escape Lucrea in public.

"It is the same as yours. I want to aid your mission to right the energies of this planet. I can best do that in your form."

"It is of the undead, what we call the Aja, the unborn. They usually leave us alone, but they desire to inhabit our bodies..." Sanda was sure he had the situation figured out.

"That is what you think. That is not what we are. " The Anila announced in Durmah's voice.

"We are the aboriginals of Vantanahan. Our race exists on another plane, in spirit form as you see it. We were here before you were planted, not so long ago. The vortex imbalance is also a crisis to our kind. I was sent to find an answer."

The others stood and let this sink in. If this was truly a planetary mission, why shouldn't all life forms be a part of it? In their ignorance and fear, they had never imagined these life forms to be a source of assistance.

"Why the body borrowing? Why the sneak attack? You must realize that it would not be well received by Durmah's friends." It was slowly dawning on Sanda that they had been wrong about these spirit forms they had sensed as time passed.

"I realize little of your kind. We are as ignorant and fearful of you, as you are of us. I saw my effect on the little one there the other night. I meant no harm, just tired to communicate. My next idea was to communicate in the form and language you understand. We have a way of taking on another's form, sending that form's operating spirit into Reyami, a dark place of waiting, holding the spirit as this body does, until it is time for it to return."

"How can we believe this is true, what you say? How do we know there is a spirit of Durmah in this Reyami?" Ede was feeling protective and concerned at the same time.

"I can allow you to communicate with it, if you like. I can send your spirit there to talk to Durmah, explain what is going on."

"All of this should have been done before, with Durmah's permission..." Sanda was mostly thinking out loud.

"That I now know. As I said, I know as little about you as you do about us. We do not live to steal your bodies, as you suspect." Here he looked pointedly at Sanda, who blushed. "I am doing my best. I can make amends."

"Well the first step would be for me to go to Durmah and let him know what we now do. He must be terrified." Ede looked at the thing that had earlier been her Durmah.

The Anila looked back at Ede and answered, "When would you like to go?"

"The sooner the better," she began and the Anila moved Durmah's body to her.

"Are you sure you feel up to this, Ede?" asked Lucrea.

"Yes, I know Durmah best and I think I could comfort him better than anyone." To the Anila, she asked, "What do I need to do?"

"Lie down and make yourself comfortable. You'll be in that position until I bring you back." Ede lied down and she saw Durmah's body kneel near her and put its hand on her head. Her eyes closed and she felt like she was falling asleep. She woke up in The Dark.

Reyami (Reyami, The Dark)

"Durmah? Are you here?" Ede's spirit sensed the dark all around, the feeling of being naked, body-less, in the vast darkness.

"Ede? Is that really you?" At first, he was thrilled to hear familiar voice, and then he heart dropped, "Are you dead, too? What has happened?" She heard Durmah's thoughts as if he were speaking them. "I don't know if I should be happy to hear another voice or sad at your being here, too."

"Be comforted, Durmah, you are not dead, you have been, borrowed, albeit without your permission."

"That presence. The last I remember, it was very near, and then, nothing. This blackness...I could feel 'me' but not my body. I'd assumed it had killed me."

"It wants to help in the mission. We are learning more about each other. It's fascinating. Taking over your body to it seemed the most logical way of interacting with us. It means no harm." Ede tried to make her thoughts comforting and reassuring in the absence of any physical touch.

"How long? Have you all agreed to this? How do I know it'll return me to my body? I miss it. I feel so lost without it."

"It is determined to be of assistance. We feel we have to go along since it is the only one who can return you to where you belong. To answer your question, I don't know how long. It depends on how long the mission will take."

"I see." Durmah's spirit was calmer in Reyami than it would have been in his body on Vantanahon. There were no needs to fulfill here, no hunger, pain, fatigue or sensation in general. Just thought and memory. He'd already grown accustomed to entertaining himself by replaying his past, his memories, like little movies, modeled on the ones he'd seen in the Archives, in the darkened room. At times, there seemed to be others near him, watching what he was remembering. Would that even be possible? For other sprits to 'see' his memories, be a part of the show? The thought of sharing popcorn entered his mind.

"It's not so bad here," observed Ede, sensing the comfort of the dark and the other spirits around - Durmah most clearly, but others vaguely, keeping their distance. "Who are these others?"

"You sense them, too? Others like me or others like them?"

"Do you mean other Anila? It's possible, I'll ask when I return. I think I need to get back. I'm feeling like a tug..."

"I'll be OK. Be cooperative. That will be the best way for me to get back to me, if it's at all possible. I will have to believe it is. I would never have believed a place like this existed in this life this time yesterday..."

"I agree. We'll try to learn as much as we can about the Anila. In the meantime, think of it as a long, overdue vacation." And then she was gone and he was 'alone' again.

"Right."

"What's it like?" Lucrea was the first to ask when Ede's body again opened its eyes and looked up to see her looking down.

"Like its name, it's dark but not scary dark, like the back of your eyes dark when you close them. There are others near, who are they? Other Anila?"

Durmah's head turned to her. "Yes, we inhabit that plane of existence, but we can also travel to others, like this one. They intersect on this planet. It is why we want to be of help, with the energy imbalance. It has become more dangerous to come here since the vortices are out of sync, and we enjoy coming here to this plane. We have lost some Anila recently; they have left but never returned to Reyami."

Ede perked up, "You didn't tell me about the risk."

"There's always a risk in travel. I decided it was worth the risk, for you to communicate with Durmah's spirit."

They were adapting to these dealings with another life form, another logic, another way to see the world, but it was a struggle, more for some than for others.

"When we get to Indrasiah, how do you see you helping us?" Lucrea inquired as she realized they themselves had not yet a plan to action.

"We'll cross that bridge when we come to it," and everyone recognized the strangeness of hearing one of Durmah's favorite sayings in a foreign accent.

The Crossing

By the time Ayah, Rander and Sen returned, the three dolphins were happily on their way to Indrasiah with their different messages. As they approached the camp, they saw Durmah at the center of the group and wondered what luck they had had in finding the Presence. As they neared, they sensed the absence of Durmah and the presence of the Presence. It didn't take many questions to find out what had happened.

"Another bit of information for the Omatra of Indrasiah?" asked Rander.

"Sometimes there's too much information. He's in Durmah's form, hopefully we won't have to explain at all."

"That would make our lives easier," Sen concurred. Then the two took to observing the Anila; the opportunity was too great for a Sensitive to pass on.

They didn't have to wait long for the Marta's answer delivered by all three dolphins at once. Ayah and Rander had been camped by the seashore waiting for the clicks which would announce the return of the Bala pod. They each chirped the same reply to the group's request.

"We will not hinder your arrival in any way. The urgency far surpasses any rules or tradition formulated in an earlier time. We only require that you all cross in the customary way, the sooner the better. After notifying the others to leave at first light, Rander and Ayah jumped into the Saragossa that night. For the first time in a few days, Ayah felt better about what he had done to save Ede and the future in general.

Swimming at night, accompanied by the playful Bala was romantic and exotic. 'It may be one of the last times we have to spend together, alone or otherwise,' thought Ayah as he swam confidently beside Rander, flanked by two Bala, the other swimming up ahead. Regardless of the consequences of his using the transfer on a mission, there was still the inspiration of death he had had on the first day.

'Will it be the swim that kills him?' wondered Rander as he evoked the Ka Daklu to keep such morbid thoughts from getting to Ayah. Ayah sensed the invocation and guessed what was behind it. He nudged Rander playfully and they swam circles around each other and the Bala, moving forward and avoiding some of monotony of the long swim. When they got tired, they hung onto the Bala, getting a free ride. They imagined the others coming this same way the next morning and doing the same thing. It was a great way to save energy.

Ayah and Rander wanted a head start also to work on the fix, which had started to nag Ayah in his sleepless hours. They really didn't have a plan and time was running out. They needed direction. But for now, they were swimming together, a destination in sight, playing and getting exercise, alone with each other turning off the finite future fears to just be in the here and now. Meteors flashed overhead, it was their season, and the warmth of the air and the coolness of the water of the sea made the seven hour crossing seem much faster and they soon collapsed on the beach, looking up at Indrasiah. Ayah and Rander asked the pod to swim back and accompany the others in the morning. Ashtu may need to ride on the back of one. They happily agreed.

"We have a growing pool of expertise," observed Rander. "More than we had imagined from the start...a meerkat, Sanda with the Adrija knowledge from the mountains, you with your origins in the forests and now the Anila, a force we hadn't even realized existed. I believe this is no accident. It will all help. Once up, we need to wait until everyone is assembled before we start anything..."

"Agreed," nodded Ayah, admiring Rander's maturity and wisdom. "And don't forget the P...it is their input that I'm interested in right now. Will you be willing to initiate them to do a program on the various causes of the current disturbance as soon as we get on top? That way, we'll be able to see what we're up against."

"Consider it done. Let's get there before midday." and Rander led the way up. There was a feeling, now that they were so close, that time was running out and they had to act quickly.

REUNION AT INDRASIAH

The others were up early the next day. Anticipation of the seven-hour swim thick in the air, Sen had tried to communicate to Ashtu what they had in store, but with little luck. It was not in her experience to swim more than a short distance, and then only under the direst circumstances. She shared an aversion to water with her feline cousins. The Anila inside of Durmah was equally unprepared. He at least understood in theory what needed to be done. Little could anyone guess that the two would enable each other to make it across, the one keeping the other, and that they would end up bonding over it...a bond that would last beyond the Anila's stay in Durmah's body.

Ede dove in first, having spent another inspiration-less dawn, with Schmanaha bringing nothing but warmth to her expectant countenance. Lucrea followed her soon thereafter, hoping to wash the continuing images of Osmand responsibilities away from her mind, envying Ede's blank slate and considering her recent advice. Sen followed them after a brief struggle trying to get Ashtu to come with him. His inspirations continued to be tied in with Ede and Rander's baby.

"Leave her to me," spoke the Anila through Durmah. "I understand her fear and can calm her." Ashtu looked into Durmah's eyes and leapt nonchalantly onto his shoulder. Durmah followed Sen leaving Sanda standing alone on the beach watching them swim towards Indrasiah.

Sanda remained standing, watching the swimmers disappear into the horizon. He had wanted to do the swim alone. He needed the time to think, to be by himself. He had spent so much time with them, with Rander especially, and all these other strangers, not to mention The Anila, not even a human, and he needed a break. He had come along on impulse. He felt he needed to be part of this mission, but he was also infatuated with Rander. He'd never met anyone so compatible. He knew Rander was bonded to Ayah, but he also knew Ayah's time here was limited. He sensed a future with Rander and that both appealed to him and scared him. Moreover, it didn't make sense.

That morning, he'd watched them all face the sun, eyes closed, with the Anila in Durmah at his side. He couldn't explain what was happening anymore than the Anila could. He closed his eyes anyway and saw himself on a ship with Rander, shooting through the stars. He'd always imagined star travel, but it had never been so detailed, so real His previous imaginings paled before what he saw behind his eyelids on that black screen, were projected images of wondrous sights and unimaginable, heretofore, adventures. With all this going on in his head, he dove in like Lucrea before him, hoping to wash it all away.

They had started climbing the cliffs to Indrasiah at night, after they had rested from their long swim. As the suns began to rise, they stopped midway to the top, clinging to the cliff walls, and faced them. Rander held Ayah's hand as they faced their destinies.

Ayah wanted to try to focus the inspiration to tell him where the death he'd seen would be coming from. Was it punishment for using the transfer? Would there be another Shitsmayeh or some unforeseen accident? Maybe he'd get in the way of a vortex out of control at Indrasiah. He closed his eyes to the first sun and had the flash, "It's part of the fix."

Rander felt Ayah tense next to him. He sensed he was getting more information on his future demise. Rander saw Sanda with him and they were on an adventure...and they were happy.

Making his mind a blank, he hoped he would not be asked to share his inspiration this morning and just then opened his eyes to the ocean. He climbed up for a better view, leaving Ayah to himself.

"I can see them swimming!" cried Rander much later from on top of the periphery rim surrounding the valley that was Indrasiah. "I can make out Ede in the lead, with Lucrea close second and Sen coming up behind and, it's Durmah, I mean The Anila with Ashtu clinging to his hair. Why is she with Durmah, I wonder? And where is Sanda?" He panicked for a moment, not seeing him. "Did he change his mind and go back to the mountains?"

"He'll come," encouraged Ayah, breathing heavily as he joined his partner on top of the cliffs. "Maybe he needed time to himself. A lot has happened in his sheltered life over the past two days."

"Thanks for understanding," Rander was looking deep into Ayah's eyes and pulled him close for a hug and kiss. "How will I manage without you? Do you really believe you are leaving us?"

"We all leave each other at some point. I can't imagine being left behind. Where I'm going, there'll be so much to see and do...yet I sense you will be well taken care of, and traveling in a parallel plane to where I'll be. Maybe our ships will pass in the night..."

"The night of eternal space – somehow it doesn't seem so scary or lonely knowing you will be out there, too." And they held on to their mortal forms as they saw the swimmers land on Indrasiah's shores.

Calling down to them, Rander shouted, "Welcome to Indrasiah. We were scouting up ahead. Go ahead and rest down there and then start the climb up. Watch out for the stickers!"

"That's an understatement!" called up Ede and she looked at her nakedness and the long climb up. They'd left their clothes back on the beach on the other side of the sea. Clothes were not allowed on Indrasiah. She'd grown up that way, but had gotten used to being clothed as well. They all had light-weight foot coverings, good for walking or climbing and waterproof backs containing their sleep gear, but nothing else. The weather was always mild here and there weren't any insects on Vantanahan, so it was usually quite comfortable to be nude. The climb up the cliffs would be a challenge, however.

Lucrea was probably the most self-conscious about nudity. 'Large bodies with their folds and curves have their own beauty,' she'd been told, but she never really bought into it. She was jealous of the lean, stream-lined bodies around her. She stared at Durmah and Sanda in covetous awe.

"You have the body of a goddess," said Sanda, sensing her discomfort. He was admiring her as well.

"Which goddess might that be?" asked Lucrea in return, doubtful of his sincerity.

"Why the fertility goddess, of course. Surely you've seen the statues and representations of the old home planet? It shows generosity of spirit." Sanda smiled.

"Listen to Sanda, Lucrea," Ede added. "You carry your weight as a woman is built to. I've seen you move and you manage it well. I wish I could manage these as well." Ede adjusted her

111

largish breasts. She herself was a bit self-conscious about being so top-heavy.

"Why do you wear clothes in the first place?" This coming from Durmah's mouth brought a smile to the women's faces. Those words had probably never been formed by those conservative lips before!

"It's custom and tradition and social protocol." Sanda, who of them all was probably the best candidate for poster child for nudity, decided to try to help the Anila understand.

"I notice the creature you call Ashtu has no need for clothes," Durmah said holding out Ashtu.

"In a way, she's already clothed in her fur. We used to have more hair in our beginnings, but over the years, lost most of it. It no longer served a purpose." Sanda explained.

"I have heard that we had forms once, too." Began the Anila. "We eventually evolved out of them, into pure light, then pure energy, which is where we are now."

It was late in the day when the second party topped the cliffs and plopped down on the soft green grass of the top plain to rest.

After four days, they were all finally arriving at Indrasiah. As the group set up camp to the Northwest of the vortex, they made efforts to respect those unsettled spirits all round and hoped that their work where would settle both the energy flow and the spirits discontent. Little did they know how the presence which had joined them via Durmah from the plains of Shawnboya would add to the spiritual melee of the moment in Indrasiah.

"What have you found so far?" asked Ede as Rander and Ayah came over to join them.

"The vortex here was the origin of the aberrant energy surges. They darted out in the four directions on a horizontal plane. Usually the vortex's energy goes straight up and out into space. These powerful surges destroy anything in their paths, as you can see in the patterns of destruction around you." Ayah paused for a second, "I have an idea what is causing this imbalance. It came to me as soon as I entered the plain."

"Sanda, we need to contact the P now. We need what information they can pick up from this damaged environment."

Rander closed his eyes, standing at the sight of the last aberrant energy blast, and made contact with Sanda, uniting the P to start their calculations, Rander's from the site of the power surge, Sanda's from the periphery. Silver sparks danced in their eyes and their companions stood by and waited to see what would happen next.

The P spread out a web-like matrix which enabled them to examine the area in detail and try to determine what was happening that shouldn't be happening-that was against the natural order of the planet. They had in their memory banks, the original energy patterns of the planet before it was terraformed or colonized. By comparing that to the present patterns, they could see how off kilter the planet had become.

"How many more will have to die before we achieve a balance?"

"We don't necessarily have to die," began Sanda, his eyes on Rander. "There are other ways we can leave. The P have already come up with an evacuation plan."

"Evacuation? Do you mean leave Vantanahon? Who would choose to leave their home?" asked Lucrea, incredulously.

"This is what came to me. There are too many of us. I don't think the P took the Anila into account when they made their plans for Vantanahon.   Some brave souls among us may have to choose to leave so others can be permitted to stay," Ayah said thoughtfully. "and some of us elders may choose to leave earlier than our regular life cycles would dictate. We only need role models, someone to take the first step, be the pioneers in this new world order." While saying these words, it became clear to him that his departure from this plane of existence may very well be voluntary. The groups split up and wandered in groups of two around the ravaged plain: Rander and Sanda, Senthion and Ayah, Ede and Lucrea and Durmah and Ashtu.

It was towards evening when everyone had reunited at the center of the camp they had set up. Each had been off on their own reconnaissance, using their special talents combined with the information obtained from the P. If they didn't fix this imbalance, the planet would right itself and not in a way particularly sympathetic to the colonists.

It was up to the colonists to balance the planet by balancing themselves, and it was up to the P, who had originally deposited the colonists here without taking into full account the powers and needs of this planet as an organism, a noosphere, to help in the fix. The fix therefore involved the relocation of the percentage of the colonists over their allotted number, a percentage which the P had just calculated to be 25%. Some would volunteer to go to other planets. Others would have to choose the earlier death option because not all 25% could be transported out.

The P reported that comet Shanti had been contacted and was on its way back to that district, but would not arrive for many years. They were quite interested in Rander and Ayah's transport capabilities, and claimed they were already working on a plan to transport some colonists earlier. All that remained would be a ship that could carry them. The raw material to build such a ship did exist on Vantanahon and the P had the technology. The colonists would be the work force.

In the meantime, there could be no more births on Vantanahon, no increase in their numbers. The Anila, as the native representative, had been trying to communicate with the organism of the planet itself to see if an agreement could be reached. It now understood these new life forms had meant no harm and had not understood the importance of balance on Vantanahon. The relative newcomers were volunteering to reduce their numbers, leave and even choose to die before 'their time' to enable life to return to the balance it had once had.

"The planet was in need of more life forms at the time we were researching it as a possible place of colonization," the P remembered through Sanda. "Most systems do balance themselves out over time and we had strict rulings about overpopulation in the Budhaun, which was very strict on population control. It is painfully obvious now that we did not sense or otherwise take into account the Anila. It seems that they are a force to be reckoned with. It only makes sense that on a planet ruled by vortexes and forces, a population of spirits would be very much part of the balance.

The reality of the Fix was just beginning to sink into the others as Ayah announced that he must return, alone, to tell the rest of the population in person. Then, he would be the first to volunteer to leave Vantanahon voluntarily, in other words... die. This departure needed to be public and executed with some ceremony. He was confident that Rosediah Shanti would preside and he was hoping to have other elders join him. The Budhaun would need to be changed. There was much to be done. He was even thinking of a name for the Ending Ceremony, the Ra Naklu, the passing, mirroring the Ka Da Klu, the joining. He would say his goodbyes tonight. He was planning to transport back tomorrow at the rising of Deshmaha. He'd be with the others for one last Inspiration.

He and Rander had so little time. They went off into the ruined gardens of Indrasiah to be alone together, one last time.

"I will be leaving, too." Rander mused. "It doesn't seem so hard. I feel honored to have had the time we did."

"You have grown much, little one." Ayah sighed, smoothing Rander's yellowish hair and sculpted body as they sat on the dead grass by a dry pond, drained by the damage. "We are both fulfilling our roles as leaders by being the first to go. It all makes sense now. Of course, once the truth is known, the world stops being mysterious and random and starts to make sense again. I only wish we could have been here together during happier times." They both looked around and sat silently for hours.

Across Vantanahon, other P were being activated. This was the plan that was spread by word of mouth. A ship needed to be built on a planet with little technology. The raw materials needed to be gathered with minimal damage to the environment. The Anila were mobilized as never before and were the liaison between the human colonists, working with the P on the far-reaching solution, that had come to be commonly known as 'The Fix' and the planet-wide organism which became known as the true Saswati. With the help of the Sensitives, the ship could be transported into space and the P could take over from there. The transporting would save a lot of energy normally required to launch a space ship. Everyone was working well together and all skills were needed.

Once the P were activated, things had happened quickly. While Rander and Sanda were piecing together the data the P were accumulating, it was a dangerous time to be at Indrasiah with the vortices still running amok.

Ashtu was the first to notice. She leapt from Durmah's shoulder, which she had not left since the swim, and sounded the alarm. Sen picked it up and translated for the group.

"Something's going to happen soon, we had better take cover!"

"Stay out of the vortex's four main directions, that's where the power surge went last time," Ede shouted and she dove at Lucrea and pushed her under a high bush, just as a quiver of air blasted over them, taking out the top part of the bush and exploding the structure farther on. The others had similarly dove for cover and they all survived the first blast. By the next blast, however, they would not be so lucky. They'd be like Durmah, lying on his back with a hole through his chest, a surprised look on his paling face. It was then they realized they had not all escaped.

You see, The Anila just absorb the energy surges they encounter, become one with them, go along with the flow. So when the alarm was called, The Anila in Durmah did not flinch, or better yet, move out of the way. It was that look of surprise when he realized the mistake as he felt the body collapse under the force of the blast. He looked up sheepishly as the others huddled around him in horror.

"Don't worry, I can fix it," started The Anila and the horror turned to wonder as they saw the tendons reconnect and the hole through Durmah's center gradually fill up with the appropriate organs, tissues and bone, concealing the grass below, which had previously been visible where Durmah's heart should have been. Ashtu was beside herself in grief, but she too slowly saw the repair job, now in disbelief and not a little fear. "I was in his body long enough to understand its structure, very complex and fragile, yet it works. I'd realized that my using his body could put it in danger, so I'd worked out a neural chemical system to repair any damage I might inadvertently cause..."

"By standing directly in the path of a vortex blast when you'd just been instructed to take cover..." mouthed an angry Sen.

"It won't happen again," apologized The Anila. "The blasts mean nothing to us, like the wind for you. I forgot where and in whose body I was a second too late."

"That's easy for you to say," blurted Ede. "What about Durmah? He could have died...or did he die?"

"The Durmah you know is a spirit safe in the waiting area. He won't know what hit him." It was spooky and more than a little funny to hear these Durmahisms come out of this mouth with that accent, spoken by The Anila. It seems that the Anila have a sense of humor, irony and not to mention, access to Durmah's brain and memory banks. "In fact, he'll be better than he was before the blast. I ...uh...fixed a few problems, while mending the hole."

"Problems. What problems? Durmah was as healthy as any of us." Now it was Ayah's turn to be concerned. He had done a health check on all the members before they left the lodge and each had come up with a clean bill of health.

"A form of what you call Cancer. It had developed in the prostate gland and would have been fatal, given your body make-up and medical technology."

"But that's impossible. No one has ever developed cancer on Vantanahon. The P saw to that..." and with that, Ayah turned to Rander. 'Of course, I would never think to look for any cancerous cells...' he thought to himself and to his friend.

Rander accessed the P and gave them the information. They were pretty much fully activated these days, observing and absorbing all that was happening around Rander and Sanda. They could be questioned directly however and they had already started research into the cancer finding and had an answer by the time they were queried. No one in the group would like it, however.

In the human body, 'cancer' cells will develop to isolate and surround a foreign agent or sometimes, stimulated, cells can develop and go out of control. Tumors and lumps result. The P reported that Saswati had introduced such agents into Vantanahon's atmosphere to randomly infect a portion of the population to reduce numbers this way. She didn't realize the population would be so courteous as to practice self-elimination or removal from the planet all together. It was a sobering thought.

"Do I have this cancer, too?" asked Ayah.

"Yes," responded the Anila in side Durmah, apparently sad, his eyes to the ground.

"So I misinterpreted my inspiration and its part in the Fix. The planet has already taken care of it." It was becoming clear to Ayah that his old patterns of thinking had led him off in a direction closer to fantasy than reality. It was becoming clear that Vantanahon was more in charge of his destiny that the Budhaun. Of course, Saswati fell under Jesicaahn's jurisdiction and she did have the ultimate say. That was no surprise.

"But wouldn't it be better for us to self-eliminate? That way, the old and those who volunteer can go of their own accord." pleaded Lucrea.

"The universe has never worked that way...random selection has always been the way." Sanda said this, putting his arm around Rander and drawing in Ayah.

"You can still use your ceremony. The deaths will be different than our usual passing. The people will need a ceremony to mark or acknowledge Saswati's reasoning and take some responsibility for its part in the Fix." Ceremony was always first in Rander's mind.

"How will the people react to this cancer?" asked Lucrea. She was starting to formulate a role for herself in this developing drama. In the Osmand option, caring for the sick and dying was an implicit, if unused, role. She had already taken on that role in Ayah's care. She knew she'd be with him at his premature, cancerous end.

"They are already reacting. The infected ones have been informed through their morning inspiration. Just as my end came to me, those who have an end coming already have seen it."

"Then why didn't Durmah see his?" asked Ede.

"He saw the flowers; could that have been a harbinger of death?"

"It has never been before, Sen," put in Ayah, "But times are changing quickly. Maybe we see our own idea of heaven in the Inspiration, notifying us that it is coming soon."

"You can always dream of 'heaven'. Everyone will die eventually, it's only a matter of time," Sanda had broken away from Ayah, leaving him to comfort Rander. "What we saw would have been my idea of heaven...traveling through the universe with the P, but it's our..." Then he looked at Rander and then at The Anila in Durmah. "Do we have this cancer, too?"

"Yes. There are no ships that the P could build in your lifetime that could carry your current pattern of life." The Anila announced and the P in Durmah and Sanda confirmed this.

"Then there is no evacuation plan for us?" Rander was taking some time to adjust here. His fantasy journey to the stars with Sanda, meeting up with Ayah's spirit on the way, suddenly took on a more realistic hue...less sci fi and more death play. "Sanda and I are facing death, too?"

"I'm afraid so...the luck of the draw," another Durmahism, but no one laughs this time.

"Surely the P can come up with something?" asked Ede.

"They are interested in our transport capabilities," began Ayah, "and when we still thought we could build a ship, we were working on the theory of a group effort to transport it into space…"

"How far to the next inhabitable planet?" This from Sen.

"The P say it's in the neighboring galaxy. It's not a possibility. There is some chatter about…" and here Rander's eyes danced with silver sparks, "encoding."

"Encoding is recording a genetic pattern for future retrieval." Sanda's P took over in the explanation. "Rander needs to reproduce with Ede to continue the P line. If his DNA is encoded, Ede would give birth to Rander – again. The same could be done for me and Ayah. It's one way of our continuing."

"There remains the question if we'd like to be born again. Some of us may choose not to…" said Ayah looking off to the cliffs surrounding them.

"I think we should be encoded." blurted Rander. "It's your old thinking that would even consider not doing so." You could tell he was getting frustrated with Ayah, feeling his own mortality in a way Vantanahans hadn't had to feel before. We're being robbed of our lives by this planet's balancing act."

"You could say that your precious P have robbed you by their inept settling of this planet," Ede's politics were showing as she continued, "It is the least they can do, to give you a second chance."

122

"Why can't they just cure the cancer? Remove it like the Anila did to Durmah's?" Lucrea was not savoring a life devoted to the dying.

"It would be undermining Saswati's plan," posited The Anila, "To undo the solution she has come up with. As it is, to allow a new life requires the sacrifice of one who has not been marked with the cancer, to restore the balance."

'Could that be my role?' thought Lucrea to herself, for now. 'I could give up my life so that Rander's son could be born, or should I say for Rander to be reborn as himself?'

"But didn't you undo Saswati's plan by curing Durmah's body of the cancer when you healed it?" asked Ayah.

"You should know it is not how healing works...to heal only a part and leave a diseased part alone. I had to heal him since I put his body in a danger he would not have put himself in and the cure involved healing all that was wrong with the parts affected, including the cancer."

"So what this means is that another person needs to die to allow Durmah to live. This could be an ongoing game of give and take, just to keep the balance set in motion by Saswati's cancer infections and our interventions."

The Anila thought about this. "It is all part of The Fix and it's seeming that we do need to all work together to make it the best fix possible, and Saswati is open to some... adjustments."

"The P have come up with a proposition to Saswati." Everyone's eyes turned to Sanda's to see the silver light show emanating outwards. "They agree it would be confusing with all the healings

123

amid infestation, people wanting to be encoded and born again, others volunteering to die to make room for a healed one or a newborn. As a compromise, the P propose transporting those willing to go to the holding place where Durmah now spends his time/space existence."

"A sort of P Purgatory. How would that solve anything? What would happen to the bodies?" Sen was trying to make sense of this proposal.

Rander's P joined in, "It would be as if they didn't exist. They'd be in extended animation, until the time when they could be reactivated. Either when Shanti returns and we can physically remove them to another world, or some factor other than old age takes someone prematurely. We have the technology to preserve the bodies for the meantime."

Everyone took a moment to let this sink in. "So," Ayah began, "could even those of us now with cancer could be put in this extended animation?"

Rander now answered Ayah as himself, "Yes, if that is what you wish."

"It was never my intention to leave before my time. The Inspiration..." then it came to the original five that they hadn't shared an Inspiration since they left the mountains. There were three new members counting Sanda, The Anila and Ashtu who didn't have the Inspiration as part of their daily tradition. Rander was preoccupied with the P inside, Ede wasn't getting them anyway, so let it pass, and Sen and Lucrea were just too distracted, Lucrea with her fate as an Osmand and Sen with looking after Ashtu and Ede to some degree.

"How could we all just have forgotten to do such a large part of our day?" Sen's eyes were wide with wonder.

"It's common when you're on a quest or uprooted in some other way to quickly adapt to a new pattern of life. We've had Sanda and then the Anila to give us advice on what to do next. Also, the P have been activated and providing their own brand of inspiration." Ayah was talking and thinking it might be grounding for everyone to do the next Inspiration the way they always had done it." Then, immediately afterwards, it would be time for him to leave. He had just decided that he wouldn't wait for the P's technology to be built or their propositions to be put into practice. He was ready to move on to the next plane. He returned his attention to those waiting and said, "It's been a long day here in Indrasiah. "Let's get some sleep and do an Inspiration at first light..." He hesitated about telling them of his departure plan. "Maybe some of our choices will become clearer then."

Here Ayah looked from Lucrea to Rander to Ede and finally to Sen. Everyone nodded and went to their sleeping compartments. Rander approached and Ayah said, "Go with Sanda. I need this night to be spent alone and in meditation." And Rander met his eyes and Ayah's heart broke with love for him and then hardened a little as Rander turned eagerly to go with Sanda.

The next morning, they all got up before first light to climb up to the top of the rim of cliffs surrounding Indrasiah, so they could catch Schmanaha's first light. Sanda, The Anila and Ashtu joined the group, having bonded with them and wanting to be supportive of whatever this Inspiration would bring. Sanda had experienced one before and Ashtu was pretty much Durmah's appendage now since she and The Anila had swum to Indrasiah's shores together.

"Ashtu is basically unaware of what is going on, but Durmah's body seems to sense in its cells the importance of this time," observed The Anila as Durmah's body turned in the direction of the rising sun.

"It's interesting that we're the same species, but our people never evolved this Inspiration. Maybe it's that they are flatlanders and the sun's rising and setting is more prominent...for us, it just appears and disappears above the mountains, but stays light after it's down for a time." Sanda's eyes were on Rander as the silver sparks flew out to meet the first sun. 'Were the P curious about this Inspiration, too?'

Ayah, resignedly, Sen cheerfully, Ede grudgingly, Lucrea conflictedly and Rander expectantly stood in a row as that morning's light crept up over the Saragossa Sea. Light brightened their naked forms as the dark behind their closed eyes lit up with images.

"These aren't inspirations, they are communiqués from an outside source," reported Rander's P to Sanda's. "Some outside source is giving them daily messages, instructing them on what to do with their lives."

"Is it this Saswati, the one that's killing them off?" Sanda's P was not privy to the data being collected through Rander's inspiration. "Have they been controlled all their lives?"

Sanda reported what he was hearing to Ashtu and The Anila, who perked up at this and began thinking about how the planet could be controlling their actions. "Are you going to tell them?" asked The Anila.

"I'm not sure. I think we need more information. Let's see what the others get."

Ayah was weary of life, as if the lure of passing had weighed upon him, drug him down so he could imagine continuing on less and less and the minute ticked by. He didn't care what the Inspiration might be. Why did it matter? Today would be his last. It was all the more shocking then when he saw, behind his closed eyes, *the Adoration of the Magi*. He'd seen the old art forms from Mahavat, much of it religiously inspired. The birth of the Messiah was often depicted, but why was he seeing it now, at this point in his life's journey?

"Ayah is witnessing the birth of a Messiah?" noted Rander's P.

"Who is s/he to save this/her people from? Saswati? Jesicaahn?" Sanda's P wondered.

"According to legend, isn't it they who send the Messiah to save the people from themselves?" explained Rander's P in question format.

"What do you get from the others?"

"At first, nothing from Ede, save frustration and self-worth doubting." He began. "Then, another view of the birth of the Messiah, this from the new mother's point of view. Does that make Ede the virgin mother?" Sen is seeing the birth from the not-father's point of view.

"And Lucrea?"

"Lucrea is seeing, is being, the lamb led to slaughter and ..."

"Yes, the child is...?"

"Ede and Sen's child is, as you may have already guessed...the Messiah."

'Such imagery. Is it prophecy or analogy?' wondered Sanda. "The P have these myths, tales, images in their memory banks. Are we seeing what the participants are seeing or the P's own translation based on their background?"

"We'll find out in the sharing," and with that, Rander's P left Rander to the rest of his inspiration and the observers watched as Deshmaha rose and a new day on Vantanahon began a day destined to be the like no other in history.

"So that's that," thought Ayah as he opened his eyes after Deshmaha had risen. He looked at Sanda and the Anila watching him expectantly. "I wonder what version of which universe they saw as the P..."

Rander walked up to Sanda and the P danced back and forth. "I don't' think the P saw the same things I did and I'm not sure why." This was communicated privately to Sanda.

"I've been listening to the background noise, I'm sensing they are withholding something they think they've found out about the Inspiration. They have not accessed this channel of our communication, so for the time being, it's secure and we can communicate on it for short periods without rousing their attention or interest." They "said" these words as they hugged and did the following embrace at arms length, looking deep into each other's eyes, behind the silver's dancing. Next, they communicated likewise to Ayah and Sen. For now, the women would have to be in the dark about the suspected P's intentions. How could they communicate what they saw? Ede was easy, nothing to say, but what about Lucrea? Could she be vague enough not to draw attention to the discrepancies the men suspected? Just as the exchange was about to occur, Ashtu signaled another surge and they all dove for cover.

"I thought you were in communication with Saswati?" shouted Sanda as he dove under a bush with Durmah's body leading the way., The Anila was not about to let any damage happen again.

"I thought it was understood, that we were taking a part in The Fix and so no more annihilations were needed," spouted the Anila from Durmah's lips, now bloodied with thorns sticking out of them.

"It's the P," noticed Ayah, "These are targeted attacks at Rander and Sanda...It's the P Saswati is after, that It doesn't trust." The structure Rander had been standing in front of lay in a smoldering ruin behind him, having dodged the blasted bullet. He looked in panic at Ayah, the Silver P flecks in his eyes not dancing for once. It was as if they had landed and were silently observing what would happen next.

Jumping at the chance, Sanda announced, "We need to deactivate the P immediately. Their presence is putting us in danger."

"Can they even be deactivated once they've been activated?" asked Ede.

"Why not? Pull the plug!?" Ayah shouted and with a look of intent in both Rander and Sanda's eyes, the silver sparks flicked out, though not totally of their own accord. The P were ultimately surprised that they had had so little power in being turned off... and they didn't even get to hear the Inspirations, though there was a sense now, as they were being turned off, that it no longer mattered.

Sanda and Rander looked lost now that they were alone, without the P's voices or presence. Ayah had already communicated to the Budhaun that the P needed to be deactivated planet-wide. This was the price of the Fix they had been sent to find. Within hours, it was done and the carriers all over Vantanahan sat alone for the first time in a long time, just like Sanda and Rander sat now.

With the P deactivated, Indrasiah was a more peaceful place to be. They had some time to rest and recoup and decide what needed to be done next. Ayah announced his plans to return to the plains and instate the Ra Naklu.

"So, without the P, we're on our now, no resurrection, Purgatory or statius," mouthed Sen as he sat with Ede and Lucrea, looking at Ayah sadly. "It was a nice fantasy to think they could have saved us...made our lives the same as before."

"All it was was fantasy, " said Ayah kindly. "We need to start to get used to the idea that our lives have changed and we can never go back. It seems the P have kept us sheltered from the world and it took this world fighting back to wake us up to the reality of our lives here."

The Anila sat back in Durmah and listened to these human creatures struggling to come to grips with their lives as they really were. Ashtu was sitting on Durmah's shoulder, the bond between the two creatures strengthening moment by moment.

"I'll be transporting soon," Ayah said, tearing up. "I'll be taking my leave of you. We need to try to explain this new reality to the masses. He turned to Rander who had come up behind him. "And you, little one, will be the hardest to leave behind."

"I won't be here long without you. Sanda and I will follow in your footsteps." They hugged. The others joined them and in the midst of the emotional moment, Ayah was gone. They felt the absence and then the loss. Lucrea ran into the trees weeping and Sen and Ede held on to each other.

"We don't die," said the Anila simply...."I can't imagine being here one minute and gone the next. How can you take it, knowing it'll happen to you one day?"

"Mostly we don't think about it. It would be too much. We are forced to face our mortality at times like these, and here on Vantanahon, we've been spoiled by the P into living lives mostly free of illness and death. Yes, we would die, peacefully and painlessly after a full life. This planetary imbalance had caused us all to realize how imbalanced our lives had become without the usual random disasters our species has been so used to dealing with." Sanda was holding Rander who was heaving and sobbing over Ayah's passing.

"What happens when the P return one day on Shanti?" Asked Lucrea as she returned from the woods.

"They'll find a world quite different from the one they left," said The Anila, surprising the others by his contribution to their discussion.

With Ayah gone, the others were left to face their own futures. With the P out of the picture, Rander no longer had a need to

131

procreate with Ede to produce an heir to carry on their work. It left him to face his end with Sanda. They would return to the mountains for Sanda to educate his people on the ramifications of the Fix.

Their mission finished, Rander was ready to transport the group back home. Until the time for Ayah's passing, the Rah Daklu, he would follow Sanda to his home. He really had no where else he wanted to be. Ede, Sen and Lucrea wanted to be with Ayah in his last days, so they returned to Ojaswan.

The Anila now understood these creatures well enough to return and exchange places with Durmah's spirit. He could still be close to both Durmah and Ashtu in his native form. As the sun rose in the sky, Ashtu nestled in her perch on Durmah's shoulder and cleaned herself as the suns' warmth comforted the unusual trio. The Anila would miss aspects of this existence, so different than its own.

Ashtu had a lot in common with the Anila, meerkat could also sense the planet's, Saswati's, needs and could warn if vortex imbalance was imminent. She had saved the group back on Indrasiah before they had figured out what needed to be done and more importantly, what they had done wrong.

Ede and Sen remained bonded by the ceremony which brought her back from death. The thought of having children still interested them. Who knows when a new life would be allowed under the complicated balancing act that was the healing Vantanahon. It would be an interesting mix of Sen's hyper sensitivity and Ede's pragmatic oblivion to the orchestrations of Saswati.

That left Lucrea and her Osmand vocation. She would first take care of Ayah, and then Rander, providing comfort to her brother and his friend as they showed the people how to die.

Her people had too long lived out of balance on a planet that required nothing more from their existence on it but balance. Life would be hard and perceived as cruel for a time, until the balance was reached again. She looked forward to Durmah's return to his body. Maybe she could be of help to him, too.

Durmah's spirit was awakened as if from a long sleep as the Anila came to fetch it and bring it back to his body. It felt as if he were hanging on a tree and some force like wind lifted him off and carried him back from the dark to the light and like slipping into his sleeping compartment, he left the world of air and re-entered his body, opening his eyes to his body lying down, surrounded by the others. Lucrea was holding his hand and the meerkat, Ashtu was sitting on his shoulder. Both felt so right and he was comforted by their presences as his mind struggled to keep calm and try to understand what had happened to him. He saw sadness in their eyes and noticed Ayah's absence. Something had happened while he was out. Rander and Sanda did not look well, but he felt surprisingly healthy and fit, almost like new.

"Welcome back," whispered Ashtu and Durmah was amazed that he could understand her now. After Lucrea and Ede got him up to speed with their current situation, he decided to accompany them to be with Ayah. He had to deal with his inability to be able to protect him from this cancer that the Anila had cured him of. He could sense Its presence and listened as Ashtu chatted with it on his shoulder.

THE RA NAKLU CEREMONY

Ayah appeared in front of the Budhaun to explain The Fix. People in the plains had had the inspiration of death and were already getting sick and so his explanation of the cause, Saswati, was not a complete surprise. He outlined his plans for the Passing Ceremony and notified them that he'd be the first to go.

"Is there no other way?"

"Was it wise to banish the P?"

"How can we make it on our own?"

These were the three most common questions. He had special meetings with those who harbored the P within. He needed them all to agree not to activate them, ever. They would have to die out with this generation. That was vital to The Fix. Without the P to signal the traveling comet, there would be no return of the Shanti. Without a signal emitting from it, Vantanahon would be crossed off as a failure and they would be left in peace on the planet of their birth. Those who had already activated their P complied and the sliver sparks were not seen again in the eyes of Vantanahans.

The Anila were invited to join the Budhaun, as were the meerkat and Saswati. It would make for a more representative body to govern the reunited planet. A complicated tally of births and deaths was established and couples wanting a child needed to apply well in advance and pass a specific test drawn up by the Budhaun to try to ensure good parenting and children well wanted.

Durmah and the others decided they would return to Nish Para Acala' for Ayah's Ra Naklu. It would help in the acceptance for the people to see the original group sent to surmise the fix in attendance.

"We are gathered here this morning to honor the chosen passing of Ayah," began Rosediah

Shanti, as she presided over the first ever Ra Naklu. It had been decided that they gather in the dark before dawn and light the way for the suns. There were candles lit and burning in front of her dais and people were individually holding candles. Ayah was standing to her right in white robes with a peaceful look on his face. His cancer had been confirmed by the Healers, but it had not yet manifested any symptoms. He saw his mission group in the front row, with Rander standing with Sen and Ede. Sanda was standing a part with Durmah, Lucrea and Ashtu. He could sense the presence of the Anila. He was comforted that Rander had chosen not to stand with Sanda for the ceremony. It would be easier that way. Slowly, as the darkness retreated, the candles were blown out by the holders and by the assistants in front of Rosediah. Ayah felt the rays of Schmanaha one last time before he saw them appearing over the treed horizon. The ceremony was held in his home forest at Nish Para Acala'. He closed his eyes, as did everyone else, for the last Inspiration he'd have on this plane. He was not surprised to see the flowers in all their calliope of glorious colors. It seemed fitting. He opened his eyes and gazed at the faces of his friends to see their expressions as they saw this day's Inspiration.

Off to the side of the ceremony, held back by Budhaun security, were a group of protestors. They believed the Ra Naklu was a form of suicide which should not be allowed by the Budhaun. Some were Ayah's family or supporters, others were religious zealots or P-supporters who did not approve of the course matters had taken on Vantanahon lately. Ayah could hear them chanting and singing in the background.

"Welcome to my Ra Naklu. I know not everyone supports our decisions regarding The Fix and we value and appreciate your dissention. I will not stoop to negativity here, as I have never used it in any of my past dealings, as my friends and family can tell you. We get what we ask for. Though I don't recall asking Jesicaahn for an earlier departure date or the need for a new ceremony, here we are, making do. I have come to believe that I truly wanted to leave this plane to go travel the stars, like our banished P." Here a murmur went through the crowd and the protestors, some of whom did not feel comfortable in a world without the P available, wailed anew.

Ayah drank the potion to stop his heart and climbed of his own accord onto the funeral pyre to be burned in a rare celebration of fire, with his ashes returning to the earth which fed his beloved trees. In doing so, he recreated another famous death performed thousands of years earlier in another time of crisis on another planet. He lay down and closed his eyes, Rander bending over him, his blond hair and beautiful face haloed by the suns light, straightening his robe was the last image he would have in his life on Vantanahon.

He felt a moment of panic as he realized the potion's effect. 'Jesicaahn! Am I doing the right thing? It is irreversible now. I don't want to go! I don't want to leave yet...' Behind paralyzed eyes which looked calm and at peace, the part of Ayah's body that was his mind grasped to hold the soul back on its way out. Fortunately Rander did not see the inner struggle and was a peace at Ayah's perceived peace.

After it was over and the ashes of the cremated Ayah scattered in another ceremony at his favorite place, the grove of trees near Rander's brother's lodge, the others parted. Lucrea went back to the mountains with Rander and Sanda. Durmah and Ashtu and the Anila accompanied them on their trip. Ede and Sen stayed behind on the plains, to help educate the people and Ede joined the Budhaun in Ayah's absence. The Anila and Ashtu promised to return to be members as well. There had been enough volunteers to do the Ra Naklu that couples could start to have a child again. In honor of their role in The Fix, Sen and Ede were granted the first privilege. Their baby would be the first to be born in to the new world order. Life would continue and after a long dark winter of death, spring on Vantanahon would bring forth new life and healing. The last attack by Saswati had been in Indrasiah, just before the group realized the need to banish the P. They hoped to name the child in Ayah's honor.

The end.

Epilogue

The soul that had inhabited Ayah's body lingered on Vantanahan to watch that body's final days. The detachment was complete. It retained all memories, including that of the body desperately trying to hold on to the soul as it exited. All the sensations of a lifetime were now recorded in the soul's memory banks as it rose up in the atmosphere to begin its journey to explore the universe. 'This was what I as Ayah used to imagine Heaven to be,' and it recalled a line from a play by an old Mahavat writer, 'Good night, sweet Prince, And flights of angels sing thee to thy rest,' as it saw the blue skies darken, the silver-green world retreat below and the suns grow larger and brighter in the darkness of space.

INTERVIEW WITH THE AUTHOR

Q: You created such an ideal world on Vantanahon. Why did you decide to tamper with it?

A: It is the fantasy that there can exist in this universe an 'ideal world' Sure Vantanahon had overcome some of the problems we are currently dealing with, but it also had its own version of global warming. The planet had already been tampered with by the P.

Q: The planet-wide imbalance. So this was a comment on what is going on in our world today?

A: Of course it is. The universe is not a safe place and will never be one. The fantasy that there is a savior out there, either in the form of a person or a machine is a fallacy. We are here to save ourselves...often from ourselves.

Q: You killed off most of your many characters. What's up with that?

A: I guess I wanted it to be real. Death is real. People die. People we have come to care for die. That's part of the pull of the story. Not everyone makes it.

INDEX: of Characters:

Ayah, Healer and Sensitive, partner to Rander

Rander, Healer and P-carrier, partner to Ayah

Raphound, twin of Rander

Edelphia (Ede), Scout and Inspiration-blocked partner to Senthion

Lucrea, sister to Rander, future Osmand

Senthion, Sensitive, former partner to Ayah, future partner to Ede

Rosediah Shanti, Spiritual leader of the Adrija' or Mountain People

Yeshmani, Creator of the Parushaha, savior of the species

Durmah, Quest Leader and future host to the Anila

Ashtu, meerkat companion to Senthion and later The Anila through Durmah

Sanda, brother of Rosediah Shanti, P-carrier, future partner to Rander

The Anila, spirit form native to Vantanahon, travels with the group in Durmah's body

of Sanskrit names (samskritam)

Vantanahon, the planet of the twin suns

The Ka's, a series of ceremonies performed on Vantanahon

Ka Daklu, ceremony of binding 2 people together

Ka Mahavat, ceremony before a journey or quest

Ka Jinbatan, coming of age ceremony

Ra Naklu, ending ceremony devised by Ayah as a part of the Fix

Parushaha, machines enabling intergalactic travel

Tandara, traditional exchange dance, reflected in the P sparks of communication in their human host

Mahavat, the Home Planet, home of Yeshmani and the name for the Planetary Energy, the Gaia of Vantanahon

Indrasiah, the First Landing Site, now a holy site on Vantanahon

Omatra, spiritual guardian at Indrasiah

The Reyami, a dark place inhabited by the Anila

Departieh, vortex on Vantanahon (A vortex is defined as a "whirling mass of something, especially water or air that draws everything near it toward its center...a situation or feeling that seems to swamp or engulf everything else."

Schmanaha, the First sun to rise on Vantanahon

Deshmaha, the Second sun of Vantanahon's suns to rise

Uravahn, the dolphin name for human life forms

Swastia, vision quest

Rhetiorma, the Healing Power

Mahantahn, heterosexual

Sumitrahn, homosexual

Hanahan, bisexual

Kayonah, Mountains on Vantanahon

Jesicaahn, the Force of the Universe

Madonahn, the plains or flatlands

Ojaswan, vital energy, the name of Ayah and Rander's settlement, home of the Budhaun

Jayhvasu, ruler or chief in charge of a Madonahn

Naha, another vortex on Planet V

Budhaun, the ruling council on V

Osmandeshvahan, the call to Vocation

Shanta, Shanti(plural) Peace, the Colonizing Comet of the P

Vaya, Spirit used to evoke and exclaim

Rapha, vortex on Vantanahon

Shitsmayeh, violent storms on Vantanahon

"Shitsmayeh Do!" "A storm is coming, take cover!"

Shitsmayeh Na, the time after the passing of a storm

Acala', one's home planet

Nish Para Acala' Ayah's home forest, scene of his Ra Daklu

Adrija', the mountain realm and people

Sandaram, the beautiful or handsome

Khaga, a trip through the stars, space travel

Sources:
1 The Wild Trees Richard Preston